Tales of the Were
Were-Fey Love Story #2

Snow Magic

BIANCA D'ARC

This book is a work of fiction. The names, characters, places, and incidents are products of the writer's imagination or have been used fictitiously and are not to be construed as real. Any resemblance to persons, living or dead, actual events, locale or organizations is entirely coincidental.

No part of this book may be used or reproduced in any manner whatsoever without written permission, except in the case of brief quotations embodied in critical articles and reviews.

Tales of the Were ~ A Were-Fey Love Story #2

Evie has been a lone wolf since the disappearance of her mate, Sir Rayburne, a fey knight from another realm. Left all alone with a young son to raise, Evie has become stronger than she ever was. But now her son is grown and suddenly Ray is back.

Ray never meant to leave Evie all those years ago but he's been caught in a magical trap, slowly being drained of magic all this time. Freed at last, he whisks Evie to the only place he knows in the mortal realm where they were happy and safe—the rustic cabin in the midst of a North Dakota winter where they had been newlyweds. He's used the last of his magic to get there and until he recovers a bit, they're stuck in the middle of nowhere with a blizzard coming and bad guys on their trail.

Can they pick up where they left off and rekindle the magic between them, or has it been extinguished forever?

The *Were-Fey Love Story* series:
1. Lone Wolf
2. Snow Magic
3. Midnight Kiss

Part of the larger *Tales of the Were.*

DEDICATION

Many thanks to all my social media friends who were so helpful in tracking down Collin Hastings for me. LOL. Especially Tammy Shaffer, Janae Mascoe, Kim Hornsby, Nyomi Finsen, Alina Chu, Jessie Collins, Tara Bolden, and Robin Giles. You guys were a great help!

Special thanks to my editor, Jess Bimberg and my friend, Peggy McChesney, who helped me whip this manuscript into shape. Any remaining errors or typos, you can just blame on me.

CHAPTER 1

North Dakota

Snow was falling and the wind was howling as the female wolf padded across the frozen landscape toward her den. It was a lonely den now, and had been that way ever since her pup—the only one she would ever bear—had left on his own quest for truth. She'd known he couldn't stay forever. Just as his sire hadn't been able to stay for very long, but oh, how she had enjoyed the short time she'd had with her mate.

He'd simply gone out one day and had never come back. That had been more than twenty years ago now, but she'd had her pup, beautiful Joshua, who had grown into a powerful young man, to keep her company. At first, she'd been the protector, but as he'd grown, the roles had reversed, and he'd been the one to set her up in this fancy, more secure den on the edge of town, backing onto the wilderness that called to her wild nature.

Evie McCann had been young, even by shifter standards, when she'd met her mate. He hadn't been one of her people, but a man of intense magic from another realm. Faerie. That's what they called his place in the universe, but she'd just thought of him as hers.

They'd had only a few short months together before he'd

disappeared, and he'd never seen his son. Evie's heart had broken at the loss of her mate, and if not for Joshua, she probably wouldn't have made it, but the little boy had his father's magic in his soul and the wild heart of the wolf that had sustained her. They'd lived rough, but they'd made it. Both of them.

And now, her son had found a mate of his own.

He'd suffered a crisis earlier in the year when unexpected magic had made him a target for evil. He'd made sure Evie was set up in a secure location before he'd gone into the wild, leading trouble away from her. It had been one of the hardest things she'd ever done—parting with her son—but there had been no other way. She was only a shifter, of low rank in the Pack that she'd left all those years ago to be with her fey mate. She wasn't strong enough to face the kind of danger that was hunting her son, much as it pained her to admit it.

She'd had to let go. The months since had been hard. She'd shifted to her furry form more and more, trying to escape her loneliness, but it didn't really help. She was very much afraid that, one day, she'd go out into the wilds and just...never come back. Never reclaim her human form. Her human life.

It was a possibility that she still feared, which she guessed was a healthy attitude. When she got around to embracing the idea, then she'd know she was really in trouble.

Things had turned around a bit recently, though. Her son had defeated those who had been hunting him and then mated with a lovely young woman who owned a farm in the Amish country of Pennsylvania. While it was a long distance from the rolling foothills of Pennsylvania to the wilds of North Dakota, they were able to talk by phone as much as they wanted, and tomorrow, Evie would get on a plane and travel to visit them, to meet her new daughter-in-law for the first time in person. She couldn't wait.

*

Pennsylvania

The flight to Philadelphia's busy airport was uneventful, though Evie's wolf half didn't like being cramped up in a metal tube with so many strange smells. Still, the reward of seeing her son again would be worth it all in the end.

Joshua was there, waiting for her, when she exited the secure zone in the airport. She hugged him hard, stifling the tears that wanted to flow at seeing her precious boy again. Even though he was well over six feet tall and mated now, to her, he would always be her little boy.

"You look happy," she told him when she finally stepped back, out of his embrace.

He smiled as if sharing a secret. "That's because I am happy."

The truth ringing in his words made her heart fill with joy. She wanted only the best for her son, including a true mate that brought this kind of sparkle to his eyes.

"Well, where is she?" Evie teased.

"Deena sends her apologies for not making the trip, but she couldn't leave the animals on their own. The little calf she took in had a problem last night, and she's been sitting with him all morning, coaxing him back from the brink. If she'd left, he probably would have died, and I have to admit, I'm kind of attached to the little fella now."

"A calf?" Evie had to laugh as Joshua took her rolling bag and started walking toward the exit.

"You'll understand when you get to the farm. It's the oddest conglomeration of critters you ever saw, but somehow, they've formed a little barn house family." He was shaking his head now, even as he smiled.

"And they aren't afraid of you?" She didn't have to say why. One didn't talk about being a werewolf out in public where any passerby might hear.

"Not anymore. I'm not sure why they've accepted me, but they have. I almost feel like the trusty old sheepdog sometimes, but I don't mind. It would've been hard on

Deena if I didn't get along with her animal family."

Evie loved the way Joshua talked about his mate. His words demonstrated the kind of consideration Evie expected of a true mating, and it was good to hear.

"Then, there's all the wedding prep going on. Deena's been doing it all on her own, but I think things will kick into high gear when her family starts arriving in a few days."

"Haven't you been helping?" Evie asked her son, frowning. "I never had an actual wedding, but I know such things can't be done all on one's own. I would think the least you could do was help your mate set things up."

Josh put his arm around her shoulders and squeezed her to his side. Her son was so tall and broad of shoulder. As big as his father now that he was grown. He made her feel petite, though at five-foot-nine, she wasn't at all short by human standards.

"Don't worry, Mom. I'm helping. I've already done more furniture moving, laundry hauling and floor mopping than I care to admit. Deena is putting everybody up on the farm, and she wanted the house cleaned top to bottom before you got here. We also had to clear out some junk that had piled up in the guest rooms and other parts of the house where we can stash guests. I even enlisted some help from the Amish neighbors to help me build a few more wooden bed frames."

Evie smiled at the idea of her handsome son working alongside a bunch of Amish men. She didn't doubt that Josh could accomplish anything he set his mind to, but he'd never really been big into carpentry. Oh, he'd done the odd repair job around the house, but he hadn't ever built furniture from scratch.

"Sounds like you've been busy," she said with approval of his industriousness. She knew her son would be a good mate, but the way he'd sounded before, she'd been concerned. Deena sounded lovely on the phone, but Evie intended to be a good mother-in-law and make sure Deena got what she needed from her shifter mate.

Deena was a priestess. Human. And part fey, apparently.

That's why their magic had meshed so well. When Josh had finally discovered his fey side—the magic inheritance from his father—he'd sought help, and that had set him on the path that had eventually led him to Deena.

Evie was glad. She hadn't told Josh much about his father because it hurt to talk about Ray. He'd disappeared before Josh was even born, and he'd taken half of Evie's heart with him…wherever he'd gone.

Maybe it hadn't been right to never discuss Ray with Josh, but it had never really been an issue until the wild magic appeared. At that point, things were so crazy, she didn't know how to bring up the topic before Josh left her to draw trouble away from her. Even so, she hadn't readily recognized the cause of Josh's sudden problem. She'd always just assumed that if fey traits were going to show up in Josh, they would have from the very beginning.

Apparently, she'd been wrong about that. She felt terrible about it now, of course, but Josh had forgiven her, and it had all worked out. Josh and Deena both tried to tell Evie that they thought it had all been part of some divine plan, but Evie still wasn't sure. She felt guilty and embarrassed that her heartbreak had prevented her from even speaking Ray's name to his son for so long.

She intended to fix all that on this extended vacation with her son and his new mate. She had brought the few things of Ray's that she still had. She would give them to Josh now, and tell him as much as she could remember about his father. They'd have time…and it was about time, too.

"Did you bring luggage?" Josh asked as they rode an escalator down to a lower level.

"Well, I had to put the presents somewhere," she replied, grinning at him.

They stopped at the luggage carousel corresponding to her flight number and picked up her bags before they left the airport. The ride was long, but not really all that bad. Evie marveled at the little bit of the city she got to see from the truck's windows before they ended up on a more rural route.

She was enchanted by the lushness of it all. Pennsylvania was a lot greener than North Dakota, even in winter. They passed through little towns and then got on a highway that buzzed past more little towns and lots of farmland that was fallow for the winter. Corrals with horses and cows could be seen from the road, and some areas had a light dusting of snow over everything.

The snow had already been falling back home for months, but here, it was only just starting to get really cold. The temperature was balmy compared to home, and the sun was shining brightly as they made their way deeper into the farmland.

Eventually, Joshua pulled up to a pretty farmhouse that was just as Evie had imagined it. White clapboard siding with a wide front porch and sprawling sort of architecture, the house had to be quite old. Perhaps a hundred years or more. It was a house with firm foundations and a storied history, she'd bet. A house full of love.

When a petite woman who had to be Deena walked out of the barn with a little black and white calf following at her heels, Evie formed an instant liking. No wonder Josh had fallen for the young priestess. She was both pretty and shy in a way that Evie knew sucked men in like flies to honey, and her aura reeked of power. Evie could feel it across the distance that separated them.

Evie met Deena's eyes as she got out of the truck, and Deena smiled. Just like that, Evie knew this young woman was a perfect match for her son. They both had that near-oppressive heaviness about them that spoke of energy and strong will. Many Alpha wolves had that kind of presence, which could be felt by their subordinates. It was what kept order in the Pack. Knowing who was strongest was essential for an orderly hierarchy.

Evie supposed it must be that way among magic users, too, though she hadn't mixed with many Others, besides her ill-fated mating with a fey warrior two decades before. Her son had that sense of strong fey magic around him now, just

SNOW MAGIC

like Ray. And Deena had a similar sort of magic around her. Thankfully, both Josh and Deena's energies were tempered with a purity of heart and goodness of soul that prevented them from using their immense power for anything bad.

Josh would have made a strong Pack Alpha, if that had been his destiny, but when the magic rose in him, that path had been closed. Evie was thankful it had all worked out for the best. Not only had her son found allies in his quest to stay alive and gain control over his magic, but he'd also found his mate.

And now, Evie was meeting her new daughter-in-law for the first time, face to face. She took a deep breath and stepped forward.

The calf made a bleating sound of distress and halted in its tracks. Evie felt her cheeks blush.

"I'm sorry. It probably senses my wolf," Evie said, embarrassed.

Deena bent down to pat the little calf on its side and then sent it off to two fluffy puffs of fur with long necks that were hovering in the near distance. Alpacas? Evie marveled as the furry adults welcomed the little calf of a different species and herded it back into the barn.

"It's no problem. They took a while to get used to Josh too." The priestess strode forward, wiping her hands on the faded legs of her worn jeans then holding one out to Evie. "I'm Deena." Her smile was as bright as her spirit, and Evie couldn't help but respond in kind.

They grasped hands, but Evie pulled the younger woman in for a hug. "Thank you for helping my boy," she whispered to Deena as they shared the first embrace of being family. Evie stepped back after a moment and just looked at Deena, smiling. "I'm so happy he found you," Evie said finally, noticing the way Deena blushed. She really was a charming young woman with no artifice.

"I am too," Deena admitted. They both turned to greet Josh. He'd finished unloading the truck and had already put Evie's cases in the house. "I made some refreshments,"

Deena said, sounding a little nervous, still. "How was your flight?"

They made small talk until they were in the house and seated around a big, homey kitchen table. They ate the fruit and cheese that Deena had prepared as a light snack before dinner, which would be in a couple of hours, after they'd caught each other up on events.

Josh had been able to talk with his mother as much as he wanted by phone, but it just wasn't the same as talking in person. He wasn't altogether comfortable talking on the phone, as a general rule, so there hadn't been too many phone calls. Just enough so that his mother wouldn't worry. She had sacrificed so much for him, she deserved that much consideration.

And now... He had a bomb to drop. There was no way around it. He and Deena had talked it over at length, and they had decided to wait until his mother was here, in their home, to tell her the news that was still as shocking to him as he knew it would be to his mother.

"Uh...Mom?" Josh began hesitantly when there was a natural lull in the conversation. Evie looked at him expectantly. "Have you ever heard of something called a Chevalier de la Lumiere?"

"A Knight of the Light?" Evie whispered. "Yes, I've heard the term. But where did you?"

"Well...I am one."

"What?"

Josh watched his mother's reaction closely. This wasn't the biggest news he had for her, but it was something that he wouldn't tell just anyone. In fact, he wouldn't have even told his mother if what he had to say next didn't depend on her full knowledge. But first, he had to see how she took this news. So far, she just looked stunned, but then, he saw tears gather in her eyes.

Aw, shit. Were they happy tears or sad ones? Or a mix of both? He didn't like making women cry. In fact, that was right up on the top of his list of things not to do in his lifetime.

He moved his chair closer to his mother. She was such a little thing compared to him. When he'd been growing up, she'd been his fierce protector. She still was, only he was taller than she was now, and a lot stronger. Things had turned around. He would protect her if he could, but some things...like the news he had yet to share...he couldn't keep from her.

"Josh, when did this happen? How did this happen?" His mother spoke rapidly, clutching his arm as he put the other around her shoulders, resting it on the wooden chair back.

Shifters needed touch—especially when they were upset. And they needed family. Josh and his mom had been a team for so many years while he'd been growing up. She'd been his anchor, and he would be there for her, he vowed, now that he was grown. As much as he could.

"I told you about my rough journey to Deena's door." Josh had filled his mother in as he journeyed from North Dakota to points all around the United States as he sought help in controlling the magic that had suddenly flared to life in him months ago. "I landed in New York City and was told to seek a man named Duncan, who, it turned out, was house sitting for a vampire friend of his." He saw his mother's eyebrows rise at that announcement but went on with his story. "Duncan is a fey warrior. A fellow Knight, though I didn't know it, then. He brought me to Deena. I think you probably noticed that her power is also like mine—fey in nature. Her grandmother many times removed is fey, and I think you met her once. Do you remember telling me that you once encountered the High Priestess Bettina?"

Evie's mouth opened in shock as she looked from Josh to Deena and back again. Then, her gaze zeroed in on Deena again, and Josh saw recognition in her eyes.

"No wonder you're so petite," Evie said to Deena. "And you have her eyes. She was a lovely woman. So kind and pure of heart. She told me..." Evie looked back at Josh again.

"She told me you would grow to be a fierce warrior on the side of the Light. And she said we would both find happiness again, eventually. I'm glad to see her predictions have come true for you, Joshua." His mother moved closer, kissing his cheek. He was glad she was happy, and a little surprised by what she'd just revealed about the High Priestess's prophecy, but he still had more to tell her.

"Well…Deena and I had some problems with some bad dudes who tracked us here. We had a bit of a fight on our hands for a while." He would not go into detail about the danger they'd faced and how close the battle had been. There were some things his mother didn't need to know. "The thing is, after everything was said and done, I…uh…" He looked to his mate for help.

"I can channel the Goddess," Deena blurted. Evie looked at her with surprise on her face. "I mean…I'm an easy conduit for Her to speak. It's why I hide out here on the farm, because the enemy would love to get their hands on me and try to pervert my magic to their own uses and deny Her my services."

Evie reached out to Deena, sliding one hand across the table. "It's a heavy burden you bear, sweetie."

Josh's heart warmed to see his mother extending her protective instincts toward his mate. There could be no better result than that the two women who were most important to him got along.

"You actually spoke to the Mother of All?" Evie turned back to Josh.

He nodded. "She offered me the choice to serve Her as a Knight of the Light," he told her, feeling again the amazing way he'd felt when the truth of that offer had hit him. He would strive to be worthy of Her trust for the rest of his days.

"And of course you said yes," Evie supplied, knowing Josh's heart as well as he did.

"Yeah, I did," he admitted. "I'm in training now and will be for a while. Duncan is my current teacher, but I was set a task, and you should know what it is."

Evie's brows drew down in a frown. "Is it dangerous?"

Josh sighed. "I don't know. Maybe." This next part was the hardest bit to tell her, but she had a right to know. "The thing is… My father is trapped in the fey realm. I'm supposed to free him and pull him back to ours so he can complete my training. He's also a Knight."

Josh watched his mother's face closely. She wasn't surprised by the news that her mate had been a Knight, but the idea that Josh believed his father was still alive brought on powerful emotion.

More tears. Dammit. Josh couldn't take the tears. He reached over and dragged his mother into a hug. He just rocked her until she calmed, looking helplessly at his own mate. Deena gave him a watery smile, but he read compassion in her gaze and knew she was glad he was there for his mother. His mate had a big heart.

CHAPTER 2

When Evie had regained a bit of control, she pushed away from her son's strong embrace. He was such a good man.

"I'm so proud of you, Joshua," she told him, knowing she needed to say that first. He needed to know how much she loved him and approved of what he was doing with his life.

"I love you, Mom," he told her in a low voice. She never got tired of hearing that, though he said it much less often now than when he'd been a little boy.

"I knew Ray was a Knight. When we mated, he felt he had to tell me because he was here in our realm for a purpose, and he had duties to fulfill. I admit, I was insecure about him not being a shifter. I'd had to give up my Pack to be with him. We moved down from Canada and found a place to live all by ourselves. Shortly thereafter, Ray said he felt it only fair that he should tell me where he went when he rushed off from time to time. It wasn't that often, but it did happen."

She remembered those early days of their mating. She'd been so happy with her fey mate, but she'd known he was keeping secrets. Her fears had almost gotten the better of her until he'd come clean, and she realized her mate was an even better man than she'd believed. He was a consecrated servant of the Goddess. She couldn't find a better man than that.

And now, her son was following in his father's footsteps.

"You said he was trapped?" Evie asked her son, his words slowly beginning to sink in.

"So I've been told. Apparently, moving between realms isn't something that happens easily. I was also told that I've been put through a series of tests to get this far. This is another one, I think."

"I actually think it's a test for both of us," Deena put in. "Our magic is stronger when we work together, and I believe that's the whole point. The Lady wants us to get better at blending our magic, so we'll be ready if, and when, we're needed."

That sounded serious to Evie, but even she had felt the rise of evil that had been building up for the past few years. She might be a lone wolf, but she still had a few connections and had heard the warnings sent out to all shifters by the Lords. She knew the *Venifucus*, for example, were back. That evil order had been silent so long they were thought to have been extinct, but in recent years, they'd resurfaced, their purported intent to return the Destroyer of Worlds to this realm and wreak havoc on all those who would serve the Light.

"I'll be honest. That sounds kind of scary, but also very wise. Though I hate to see either of you in danger, I know you're both strong and will do your best to serve the Lady," Evie told them. "I don't have to like it, but I also agree that you two should train to make yourselves as prepared as you possibly can. It couldn't hurt, and it might just save your lives...and us all."

"Then, you're aware of the bigger picture?" Deena asked shrewdly.

"I have friends. I hear things, even though I run alone," Evie responded. "Now, tell me more about freeing Ray."

What followed was a long discussion about what the young couple had come up with. Evie was ready to give it a whirl right that minute, but the moon would be full the next night, and that was when they were planning to try. It made sense, Evie guessed, though she was no expert on magical workings. She was a shifter, plain and simple. Any magic she possessed was an innate part of being what she was. She didn't wield magic like a mage—or even like her son and his new mate did. That kind of thing was well above Evie's pay grade.

The rest of the evening passed in a blur, and when it was time to go to bed, Evie sat awake for a long time, just smiling. Ray was alive! She had something to live for again!

Evie had wondered what was to become of her now that her son had found his own happiness. Evie hadn't wanted to horn in on the youngsters' happiness. She had planned to stay in North Dakota all alone but for a few human friends who had no clue she was a shifter. She'd honestly had no idea what the future might hold, but feared it was going to be a great deal of loneliness. She didn't blame anyone for that. She'd done her job. She'd raised her son the best she could, and he'd been fortunate enough to find happiness. She didn't begrudge him that, but she wasn't that old. She wasn't ready to pack anything in just yet.

For one thing, shifters didn't age like humans. Evie wasn't even fifty yet. She probably had another two centuries left to her lifespan at the very least. The thought of facing that alone had worried her. Losing Ray meant she had already lost her one shot for true love in this world. Werewolves mated for life, and her mate had been lost long ago. There would never be another great love in her life.

But now...maybe all was not lost. Suddenly, she had a shot at happiness just one more time. A chance to live again with the only man she would ever love...if he still even remembered her.

All those old insecurities about mating with a non-shifter rattled around in her brain. Ray had tried to tell her, many times, that he felt the same bond, but she wasn't sure if she really believed it. She hadn't been sure back then, and now—after all this time—she still wasn't sure now.

The only thing she was completely certain of was that Ray needed to be free. They needed to spring him from the trap and bring him back so he could at least be here for his son. The two had never met, and it was about time Joshua got to know what a wonderful man his father was, first hand.

As for Evie... If something could be salvaged of their relationship, she would be over the moon. But if twenty years apart had soured her fey lover on their relationship, then she'd have to accept that, even if it broke her heart into a million pieces.

The next day was a little bit like torture for Evie. Not being with her son and his mate, but the waiting. That was driving her nuts. Deena was patient with her, giving her a tour of the farm and introducing her to the animals that dared come near the new predator on the property. The livestock had already come to some sort of arrangement with her son, but she was a different story. The younger horse was watching her carefully as she walked around with his mistress—as if he'd come charging to Deena's rescue should the wolf-woman put a toe wrong.

Deena's menagerie was like no other barnyard community Evie had ever seen. The animals here were magic-touched. That was the only way she could explain it.

By the time moonrise drew near, Evie was about to go out of her mind with nerves. The three of them trooped out to the copse of woods on one side of the property, and Evie was impressed to find a small circle of standing stones. A sacred circle, hidden in plain sight, in the protective woods. The magic was strong here, and as the moon rose, the two fey-touched youngsters began working spells and calling on the magic of other realms in order to free Ray.

Evie watched from the periphery, standing just inside the stone circle. She could feel and also see the forces gathering—forces she had never witnessed in such abundance before. The power her son and his mate wielded put her in awe, and she almost dropped to her knees when a huge crack sounded within the circle, and the scent of a place...not Earth...wafted through a blindingly white rift centered on the altar stone in the middle of the circle.

It smelled of flowers and Springtime. Strange spice and…brimstone?

Evie saw him step through from the portal from another realm. Her mate. Her Ray.

Then, all of a sudden, chaos erupted all around them. Ray bounded off the altar stone, looking around quickly. He saw her, and his motion never faltered. He was coming right to her, his expression thunderous as Evie suddenly realized they were under attack.

Something had followed Ray out of the rift. Something evil that reeked of smoke and putrid fire. And that thing was fighting with Josh and Deena, even as Ray reached Evie.

Sir Rayburne wasn't really sure what was going on, but something—a very strong something—had pulled him into the mortal realm. Unfortunately, it had also dragged the unholy creature that had acted as his jailor along.

Ray didn't want to stick around to find out if the mages that had freed him were good or evil. If they were good, they might possibly be able to handle the flame creature themselves. If they were evil, he hoped it ate them.

If he hadn't spotted the one familiar face he most wanted to see, he would have spent more time getting the lay of the land, but as it was, he had to protect his mate, first and foremost. He made straight for Evie—his beloved Evie.

He wanted to weep with joy, but there was no time. He had just enough magic left to get her to safety. Little Evie had no protection against the sort of evil the flame creature could produce. Better to let the mages fight it out with the beast while Ray protected the one woman for whom he would happily give his life.

He ran straight to her and scooped her into his arms, expending the last dregs of his magic to transport them both to the place he'd been dreaming of for so long. A blinding flash of light, and then, they were there. He could feel the bite of the cold North Dakota winter night. It had been summer in the fey realm, and he wasn't dressed for snow, but it didn't matter. He had his mate in his arms for the first time in way too long, and now, they were home.

Evie blinked a few times after the second flash of light. Ray still held her tight, but they weren't in the warmth of the magical circle anymore. He'd done something. Taken them somewhere. She took a quick glance around and had her answer. They were hundreds of miles away from where they had just been.

Evie clouted him on the shoulder. "Ray! What did you do? Why are we *here*?" She didn't give him a chance to answer her questions but rushed ahead, in a state of near-panic. "We need to go back and help Joshua!"

"Who's Joshua?" Ray asked, puzzled.

That stopped her cold. She looked up into his beloved face, meeting those eyes she'd thought she would never see again, and her heart just melted. He'd missed so much. He didn't even know he'd had a son.

"Ray, you've been gone a long time," she began, having some recollection that time passed differently in the fey realm than here.

"How long?" He traced the lines she knew had formed on her face in the time since he'd left.

Lines of worry, though she didn't age as humans did. She suspected she didn't even age like shifters did. Not since joining her life to Ray's. She didn't seem to get older anymore, though her experiences had aged her in ways that were visible sometimes.

"It's been more than twenty years," she told him in a gentle voice. "That man back there. That was your son. I named him Joshua. And the woman with him was his mate, Deena. They're newlyweds, and they're the ones who were tasked with freeing you and pulling you back into the mortal realm." Ray looked stunned. As well he should. Evie reached up and took his cheeks between her two hands, knowing tears were leaking out of her eyes. "I didn't know what had happened to you. I didn't think I'd ever see you again."

"Oh, Evie," he whispered, clutching her to his chest as he hugged her tight. "I'm so sorry. I never intended to leave you all on your own." He kissed her then, a kiss that tingled with his magic and innate goodness. She'd missed that flavor of power and frisson of electricity that zinged between them whenever they touched. He drew back after a moment and looked incredulous. "We had a son?"

She laughed through her tears. Incandescently happy for the first time in over two decades.

"Yes, we had a son. A big strapping werewolf with amazing magical abilities, and a new mate." She patted his chest, loving the reassuring beat of his heart under her hand. "Ray, we really need to get back to them. They may need our help."

His eyes narrowed in concern. "I can't. Not yet. I need a little time to build up my strength. I've been drained of magic every moment I was away. That creature that came through with me was literally sucking my magic out of me. The enemy laid a trap and left the creature to guard and feed off me until I was no more. I thought I might die there. Even fey can die if all of our energy is stripped away."

The horror of what he was describing pained her. He'd been through an ordeal. They'd both lost time together and so much more. She wasn't sure they'd ever be able to recapture those lost years, but she was willing to try if he was. But that talk would come later. Right now, they had to figure out how to get back to Josh. Though it sounded like that was a non-starter.

"How long before you can poof us back to where we were?" she asked.

"Poof?" he repeated, smiling a bit at her choice of descriptor. She just raised her eyebrow, waiting for a straight answer. "A few hours. What time is it now?" He paused to look up at the cold, starry sky. "Around midnight?" She nodded confirmation. "Maybe by dawn," he told her, and she realized they weren't going to get back to the battle in time to make a difference.

She thought Josh could probably take care of himself, but a mother always worried. Still, she had to be practical. She looked around and realized where they were.

"Why'd you bring us here?" she asked, curious.

"It was the only place I could think of on the spur of the moment. It was where I was happiest." He moved back, letting her go, and looked around at the cold cabin a few yards away.

They were standing in front of the home they'd shared for those blissful months when they'd been newly mated. Remote and wild, nobody lived nearby. Not for miles and miles.

"You don't live here anymore?" Ray asked, frowning.

"I still own it, but I moved closer to civilization after Josh started roaming on his own. This place holds a lot of great memories for me. We did okay here, even if we didn't have much." Josh had been raised on the outskirts of human society, always the outsider looking in, but he'd been a good boy who was always wise beyond his years.

"That must've been tough. Evie, I'm so damned sorry. I should've been here for you." He came over and grasped both of her hands in his, looking deep into her eyes. She could see his pain reflected there.

"Well, you're here now, and it seems we're stuck here for the night at least. Let's go inside and see if we can get the fire going. It smells like snow." She made light of the serious moment, because the tension had been drawing out between them in an uncomfortable way. Seeing him again, after all this time, made her feel awkward as a teenager with her first boyfriend.

But why? He was her *mate*, after all. This should be easier, shouldn't it?

Of course, he wasn't a shifter. Maybe if he had shifter instincts like hers, things would be easier. Then again, maybe not. This was all new territory to her, and they would have to figure it out as they went along.

First things first. Shelter, light and heat. She'd see what

19

she'd left behind in the way of provisions after they got those out of the way, though she was confident there'd be something. Josh had started making sure the cabin was restocked every year, in case they wanted to come up here. They hadn't yet, but every year, Josh had made the pilgrimage on his own to keep the place in good working order and ready for them.

CHAPTER 3

Ray followed Evie into the cabin. She hadn't changed a bit since he'd been gone. Oh, there was pain and sadness written on her face, but he was certain his own image held the same. Being apart from her had been the worst punishment he'd ever experienced.

The evil that had trapped him in faerie had essentially tortured him, but not being with Evie had made it all much worse. He knew shifters mated for life and that Evie was connected to him in ways he could only imagine, but he'd discovered he really needed her as much as she had probably needed him. If she was linked to him, so was he linked to her. A miracle that he hadn't expected, but treasured, even though it had caused them both pain while they were apart.

And she'd given him a son. All on her own. Poor lass. That had to have been tough. There was very little he could do to make it all up to her now, but he was going to try. He was amazed she was even talking to him after his disappearance so long ago.

Twenty years! It hadn't felt that long in faerie, but of course, time flowed differently there. He should count his blessings, because if he'd been subject to that power-draining trap for more than twenty years, he'd have been dead long ago. Apparently, he'd been in a pocket of the fey realm where time passed much more slowly. Lucky for him.

The cabin had a dusty smell, but it looked just as he remembered it. Same gingham curtains, same wood stove, same rustic wood furniture. Tarps covered the upholstered furniture to keep the inevitable dust from collecting in the fabric. He snagged an oil lamp from the table next to the door and found the matches they'd always kept alongside.

He lit the first lamp while Evie was already bustling around near the wood stove, building up a fire. She could see in the pitch dark of a North Dakota night much better than he could, after all. Werewolves were talented that way.

"Somebody must've been here recently," Ray observed, looking around the place. "There are plenty of supplies."

"Josh comes up here every autumn and makes sure it's set for the winter, just in case. He was hiding out up here for a week or two before he went east and eventually ended up in Pennsylvania with Deena." Evie was concentrating on getting the fire going while he wandered around checking out the cabin.

"What led him there?" Ray wanted to know. "And why did he leave you on your own in the first place? Growing pains?"

"You might call it that." Evie sounded just a bit sarcastic. "Ray, he was a plain old garden-variety werewolf most of his life, but then suddenly, something changed, and he had all this barely-controlled magic to contend with. He was in serious danger from unscrupulous mages who hunted him to try to steal his power. Josh left to lead them away from me and to try to find someone to help him figure out what had happened and how to control his rogue power."

"Damn. I'm sorry." Ray sat on the nearest chair. His son had needed him—probably many times—and he hadn't been there for him. He was a terrible father. He thought about that for a long moment while Evie turned back to the little flame she was coaxing into life in the fireplace. After a long moment of self-recrimination, he sighed. "Sometimes, it happens that way. A triggering event occurs, and dormant magic flares to life. If I'd been here, I could've helped him through it. Protected him while he was working on control and shielding."

Evie left the fire, which was well on its way now, and sat across from him. "You're probably not too late for that," she told him, raising a tiny bit of hope in his heart. "The reason Josh was told to break you out of faerie was so that you could help train him."

"Train his magic?" Ray nodded. "Yes, I can definitely help him with that. But who told him where I was? I didn't think anyone knew."

"There is one being who always knows, Ray." Evie's voice dropped to a respectful whisper.

"You mean…" Ray wasn't sure, but it sounded like his son had encountered the divine.

"The Mother of All spoke to him. More than that, She asked him to serve as a Knight of the Light, and of course, he agreed. Sir Duncan has been training him until Josh and Deena could break you free. Deena is a priestess and also has fey blood. Between the two of them, they figured out how to pull you back into the mortal realm."

"My son, a Knight?" He was awestruck by the very idea. He'd missed so much, but he might yet be able to build a relationship with his son as an equal—a comrade in arms, in service to the Light. It was a humbling thought.

"He's a good man," Evie said quietly. "Just like his father." She reached out, touching Ray's hand resting on the arm of the chair. He felt the impact of her gentle touch all the way to his soul. Moving slowly, he captured her hand with his and twined their fingers together.

"I've been a terrible mate, Evie," he admitted. "I abandoned you when you needed me most."

"Through no fault of your own," she insisted. "Even before I knew what had happened to you, I knew you would never have left me like that on purpose. I thought maybe you'd died, but the connection between us made me think you were alive…somewhere. I tried to track you, but I failed many times. Now, of course, I know why. Even my wolf can't track across the realms to faerie." She let out a wry chuckle. Her tone was soft. Forgiving.

Ray wasn't sure he deserved forgiveness. He wasn't really sure of anything right now, except his mate's soft hand in his. He was so damn tired, he wasn't able to make much sense of anything, but he was free. That, at least, he knew. Unless he was dreaming again...

"This is real, isn't it?" he asked suddenly, needing to know.

Tears sprang to Evie's eyes, and she squeezed his hand. "It's real. You're here, with me, Ray."

"It's almost too much to believe," he whispered. He felt an answering wetness gathering behind his eyes. Tears. He'd given in to them a time or two in his life, but he'd never allowed his captors to see his grief. He'd been strong for so long...

"I know." Evie's voice came to him as she moved out of her chair to kneel beside his.

He realized his hand was trembling. In fact, his whole body was shaking, just slightly. Fatigue had finally caught up with him, and if Evie promised him he was safely away from his enemies, he would trust her. She was the only person in the world he would trust. He could finally rest and try to recoup the power that had been drained from him for so very long.

"Come with me, my love." Evie's soft tones beckoned him to rise, her strong hands supporting his trembling limbs as she guided him over to the bed. *Their* bed.

How he'd longed to see this cabin again. The bed. The woman...his beloved mate. He'd missed her so much.

Ray wasn't sure if he was speaking his thoughts aloud as Evie tucked him into their bed. He was shivering until she climbed in beside him and wrapped her arms around him, sharing her warmth. Evie was always warm—a gift of her shifter heritage—and more than just the physical, she warmed his heart, as well. The bond between them pulsed with caring. It was beautiful to his magical sight. He'd missed this closeness he'd never felt with another being. He'd missed *her*. He'd missed so very much...

Evie realized Ray was a lot weaker than he'd let on. She would bet he'd been running on adrenaline since he entered the mortal realm. It had gotten him this far, but it was clear to her that he was about to crash.

The shaking in his limbs worried her, but that might just be cold. She remembered he hadn't always handled the winter chill as easily as she had. His clothing was thin. As if he'd been living in a summer climate. Who knew how the weather worked in faerie?

She was just glad to have him back at long last. She sent a prayer of thanks heavenward to the Mother of All, praying also for the safety of her son and his mate, and the return of health and vigor to Ray. Evie had a lot to be thankful for, but also a lot to worry about.

As Ray's tension started to ease, and he settled peacefully in her embrace, she realized that, for this moment in time, all was right with her world. It might not be perfect— particularly since she didn't know the full extent of Josh and Dina's troubles back in Pennsylvania—but as she'd often told her son, perfection was overrated. Doing the best you could was good enough most of the time, and right now, the best she could was pretty darn good.

She had her mate in her arms for the first time in decades, and her inner wolf was happier than she had been in all that time. Things weren't perfect. Not yet. Maybe not ever. But they'd work on it. They had a lot to iron out when he woke and many plans to make.

For one thing, she needed to check on Josh. Her connection to her son never wavered, so on an instinctual level, she knew he was still alive. That was comforting, at least. Whatever had happened after Ray poofed them away from the stone circle, at least Josh was still living.

As if thinking about him conjured him, Evie felt her cell phone vibrating in her coat pocket. She hadn't bothered to take off her coat since the cabin was still cold. She fumbled around to find the pocket for a moment, then was able to hit the button to answer the call. She kept her voice low, but Ray didn't stir. He was asleep. Or maybe unconscious. She wasn't exactly sure which, but her wolf senses told her he was mostly okay. He just needed time and rest to recover his strength.

"Josh?" Evie answered the phone, knowing it had to be her son calling.

"Are you okay, Mom?" Josh's voice sounded so good in her ear.

"Yeah. How about you?"

"We're fine. It got a little hairy for a bit after you guys left, but we handled it. Everything's secure. Where the heck are you?"

"Honey, Ray didn't fully understand the situation. He saw me, and I guess he felt protective. He used one last push of magic to bring us to our old cabin. We're here now, and he's down for the count. He said the creature that came through behind him was his jailor. It was siphoning off his energy a little bit at a time. We would've come back to help you, but he didn't have the power. He's asleep now." At least she *hoped* it was a normal sleep. She didn't really have any medical training and couldn't do much for him way out here in the middle of nowhere by herself if he needed medical intervention. All she could really do was pray.

"That's all right, Mom. Between us, Deena and I were able to send it back where it came from. I'm sorry if we scared you."

That was her boy, always taking on the responsibility for those around him. If they'd been in a Pack, he would've been a good Alpha, but he'd always had too much of his father in him to do well in Pack life. She'd understood that from the beginning. She'd left her Pack—where she'd been of somewhat low rank—to be with her mate. Evie had never been very dominant and was more of a lover than a fighter, which meant she didn't stand very high in the Pack hierarchy. But she'd been okay with that. She understood her place and accepted it.

Ray had changed everything. With him, she'd felt complete for the first time in her life—as if she *fit* somewhere...with someone. They'd formed a Pack of two, which had been good enough for her.

After Ray disappeared and she realized she was pregnant, she'd lived for the tiny life inside her, and Joshua had become her Pack. They'd done well together, but he'd had to leave when his magic flared out of control.

She'd prepared for a life alone, never dreaming Ray would—or even could—return. Now, here he was, with her. She almost couldn't believe it. This was her most fantastical dream come true.

"Thank you, Josh," she choked out, hoping her son would realize the tremendous emotion contained in those simple words.

"I'm glad it worked out." His low, serious tone told her he understood. Her boy was a sensitive soul. "Call me if you need me. Otherwise, we'll talk again in the morning, okay?"

"We should be fine for the night. You stocked the cabin with everything we could need. I've got the fire lit, and it's already warming up."

"Good. Deena says goodnight, and we'll speak again tomorrow." He paused. "You're sure you're okay?"

His concern made her smile. "Yes, worrywart. I'm with your *father.*" Her voice wavered with joy. She cleared her throat so she wouldn't burst into happy tears. "Truly, Joshua, I couldn't be safer. Ray is... Well...he's something special. You saw. His first instinct was to take me to safety, despite how drained he was."

"That says a lot for him," Josh admitted. "But is he strong enough to defend you if something dangerous comes to call?"

"Honey, we're in the middle of nowhere. Nothing's going to sneak up on me, of all people. I'm still a wolf. You know how sharp my hearing is, even in human form. And if I really need help and Ray can't handle it—which I'm sure he can, because he can handle just about anything—I can go wolf and run to the reservation. The shaman there should be able to lend assistance."

"Promise me you'll do that at the first sign of trouble. And call me. Just hit the speed dial. I'll answer any time, day or night."

"I know that, son. Joshua…I love you so much. You've given me back my life." Her voice broke, this time, with emotion she couldn't suppress.

"It's only fair. You gave me life. I'd do anything for you. You know that, right?"

"I do. And what you did tonight… I don't have the words…" Yeah, the tears were coming, and she wasn't going to be able to hold them back much longer.

"It's okay, Mom. I know. I love you. Have a good night and stay alert. Call me if you need me."

"I will, worrywart." She hiccupped as she laughed, and they hung up on a good note.

Then, the tears came.

Evie wept silently, her joy overwhelming her for a bright moment where her heart expanded beyond its capacity to hold in the feelings. She held on to Ray, warming him with her body, stroking his muscled arms, cherishing the fact that he was with her again. She listened to him breathe and rested her ear over his heart, reassured by the steady beat.

She fell asleep that way. In the embrace of her mate. The only man she would ever love.

CHAPTER 4

In the darkest hours of the night, Evie woke to a warm embrace. Someone was placing little kisses all over her face. Gentle touches that she remembered from long ago. Ray.

She opened her eyes to discover that, for once, it wasn't a dream. Ray was looking down at her, his smile warm and tender, his jaw firm and bristled just slightly with a day's growth of beard. She loved the feel of that stubble against her palm as she reached up to cup his cheek.

"I'm so glad this is real," Ray whispered, echoing her thoughts. They'd always been in tune like that.

"Me too." She smiled up at him. "I missed you so much." Her voice broke on a sob.

Strong hands lifted her so that she was sitting across his lap while he leaned back against the headboard of the bed. Their bed. The bed their son had been conceived in. The bed she'd felt so alone in after Ray had disappeared.

Ray ran his hands down her spine, offering comfort while she clung to him.

"I thought about you every day we were apart, Evie," he told her. "I never knew loneliness like that before, and I pray to the Goddess I never will again. I hope you don't have any plans, because I don't intend to ever let you out of my sight again, sweetheart." His words sounded only half-joking to her, but she didn't mind at all. She understood the instinct to want to keep the mate close and never let go.

"I don't want to let you out of my sight either. Not for a good long while. If ever," she told him, smiling as her tears faded. Ray was her sunshine in the dark, her heart, her life.

"Then, we're in agreement." Ray nodded solemnly, but his blue eyes were dancing with a teasing light. She loved the way he played with her. The wolf enjoyed games—especially tackling her mate to the bed and having her wicked way with him.

Which sounded like a really good idea at the moment.

Feeling both playful and a little bit shy, Evie leaned down to kiss her long-lost mate. This kiss was a lover's kiss, a passionate meeting of the lips that both knew was a prelude to more. At least, she hoped he knew. She thought he did. The hardness beneath her gave every indication that he knew.

Evie had never been truly aggressive in bed. Wolf though she may be, hers wasn't the dominant sort of animal that led Packs. No, her inner wolf was more apt to cuddle than attack, play than annihilate. That might have made her a bit more timid than most werewolves, but Ray had fallen in love with her while she'd been even shyer than she was now. He'd helped her gain confidence in herself, and then, the years when she'd been struggling without him had taught her self-reliance in a way she wished she'd never had to learn.

But he was back, and the hardship was over. It was time, now, to reclaim what she had lost, to see if their relationship could resume. It was a big step, but she wanted with all her heart to show him the woman she had become...and the fact that she loved him now as much as she ever had.

She deepened the kiss, and he followed where she led. She'd never really led them anywhere before, so this was new and exciting to her. Ray's encouraging caresses made her even bolder.

She tugged at the fabric separating their bodies. She wanted it gone. She wanted to feel Ray's skin against hers. She wanted to stroke him all over and rub herself against her mate.

He complied, getting them both naked in record time while she kissed and explored him. He hadn't changed much from her memories. He was a bit skinnier, of course. Being held prisoner could do that to a person. But he was still her Ray. Her lover. Her mate.

She pushed the blankets away and didn't really care that they landed on the floor. The only thing that mattered right now was Ray. Kissing him. Loving him.

She ran her lips over his skin, noting the spots where he had bruises. She kissed them gently.

"When did this happen?" she asked in a hushed whisper, pausing at a purplish bruise over his ribs.

Ray sighed. "My jailor would occasionally toss me around a bit," he explained, breaking her heart all over again for what he'd been through. "But don't worry. I'm pretty tough. Nothing's broken. Just bruised."

"Oh, Ray..." She felt tears threatening.

Ray took command of the situation, rolling them so that he was leaning over her. Their eyes met and held.

"I'm all right, Evie. All that is over with now, thanks to you and our son...and his mate." He shook his head a little, a soft smile blossoming. "Have I told you how incredible I feel when I think of us having a child? But he's grown into a man without my ever seeing it. He's mated." Ray looked away, strong emotion on his chiseled features. "I'm more grateful than I can say that they were able to liberate me, but I missed a lot."

Evie cupped his cheek, drawing his gaze back to hers. "Josh missed having a father, but I know our son. He's going to be so glad to know you, Ray. You can both make up for lost time. I'm sure of it."

"Maybe so," he agreed after a long pause. He looked deep into her eyes. "Are you as forgiving, Evie? Are we going to be able to make up for lost time, as you put it? Can we pick up where we left off?"

His words gave her hope and allowed that little demon of

daring to rise up again. "Do you mean from twenty years ago? Or from, like, two minutes ago?" She smiled at him, licking her lips provocatively. "Because I'm all in favor of the two-minutes-ago thing. I didn't mean to get sidetracked into sad territory. Right now, I'd like to get back to the pleasure zone…if you're willing." She lowered her eyelids, peeking at him from beneath the fringe of her eyelashes like the timid wolf that lived inside her.

Her heart filled with joy when he smiled. She remembered that expression on his face. It was the one he wore before he pounced.

And pounce he did. Ray dove in for hot kisses that nearly melted her bones. Within seconds, they were back to the sexy place they'd been before she had allowed herself to be distracted by his bruises. Maybe it was better to let him lead the way, this time. She could let her inner bad girl out some other time, but for now, she just wanted him. Any way she could get him.

Ray didn't disappoint her. Not in the least. He guided her body into the rhythm she remembered so well. The feelings she'd missed for so long. The mate she had mourned had been returned to her, and that miracle fueled a hard and fast orgasm that took her by surprise. They hadn't even really gotten started yet.

Embarrassed, she looked at his face, but Ray was smiling with satisfaction. "I see you've got a hair trigger after so long apart. That's good, sweetheart, because so do I. Once I get inside you, I doubt I'm going to last, but I promise I'll make it up to you." He kissed her, and she could feel the slight quiver of his muscles, as if he was holding himself in check, barely restrained.

He moved over her fully, and she made space for him between her legs.

"There's nothing to make up," she whispered to him. "I'm already way ahead of you."

She giggled, warmed by his answering chuckle. They'd always been able to laugh and play. Both her human and wolf sides liked that about their mate. He brought such joy to them, on every level.

He joined them together, and it was magic in the purest sense of the word. Not the magic that came to Ray so easily as part of his fey heritage, but the more intimate magic that had always flared between them from the first. The magic of two souls perfectly matched. The magic of love.

When he slid home for the first time in years, she felt complete. It was such a perfect moment, they both stilled, just breathing for a moment, looking deep into each other's eyes as the sparks of their union danced around them, bathing the little cabin in golden light. It had been so long. She'd forgotten about the fireworks.

"Who needs a nightlight?" Ray scoffed with that delectable humor he had always brought to their moments together.

She remembered all over again that his night vision wasn't nearly as acute as hers. Wolves—and most other shifters—could see well in the dark, when their predator halves made up for more human weaknesses. She had to giggle, and that slight motion set off a round of joyous sparks in her body—and in the room.

"Oh, honey," he whispered, his face smiling, but his eyes intense. "Do that again."

His almost teasing tone made her laugh harder, and then, neither of them had the breath to laugh as he began to move within her.

The rhythm was a bit more hectic than she remembered, but it was appropriate to the moment. She had missed him so much, and it was pretty clear he'd missed her, too, if his enthusiasm was anything to go by. She felt like a goddess. A femme fatale who had power over men and their desires.

Truth was, she didn't want power over any man. Not seductive power. But knowing that she could affect her mate this way reassured her inner wolf and her human heart at the same time. Some things didn't need words to prove. Some things could only be understood by actions, and this encounter was proving to her beyond the shadow of a doubt that not only was Ray still her mate in every sense of the word, but that he believed it too.

She'd been so worried that their time apart had made his fey heart grow distant, but she'd been wrong. Making love to her mate was as explosive as it had ever been, and the care he took with her—even in his frenzy—made her realize that he felt the same.

It was wonderful. Truly fantastic. Mates reunited in the best possible way. As it should be.

She came, screaming his name, only a split second before he totally lost it, burying himself in her and letting out a guttural groan of extreme pleasure near her ear. Her climax went on and on, tearing through her, stimulating senses that had been dormant way too long.

The light in the cabin grew to an intense explosion of golden sparks, swirling around them, with their union as the focal point. The eye of the storm. The center of the whirlwind. Evie watched it in wonder as pleasure splashed over her in a wave, breaking and sweeping her along in the maelstrom. It grew and grew, so intense that she had to close her eyes against the bright flare of magical sparks in the room...and in her body...and her heart.

Ray collapsed on top of her long moments later, but she didn't mind in the least. His weight was a reassuring presence. A warm blanket of security for her mate-starved senses.

Stars! How she'd missed him!

"I'm not even going to ask if that was all right," Ray said, many minutes later, after rolling most of his weight off her. He wrapped his arms around her and cuddled her into his embrace, holding her as if he'd never again let her go.

"That confident, are you?" she asked with a languid sort of pleasure still running through her body. Ray had definitely put a smile on her face that might never leave.

He shrugged, lifting her up slightly where her head rested against his shoulder. "Maybe optimistic is a better word?"

"You always were a glass-half-full kind of guy," she teased

him, stroking his chest with her fingers, glad to be able to touch him at will. "But in this case, your optimism is definitely well placed." She leaned in to kiss his neck, biting gently. "I may not be able to move for a week."

He chuckled, a satisfied sound. "That good, eh?"

Evie swatted him gently, nipping his shoulder. "Don't get overconfident. There's always room for improvement." She looked around the cabin where the light show had finally dissipated, only small motes of golden sparks floating here and there around the walls. "Of course, if we get any better, we might just blow the roof off this old place."

Ray laughed then rolled, tackling her and placing her under him again. His gaze met hers, and she could see a renewed interest flaring there. Her own body began to heat in response. She was always ready to play with her mate, it seemed.

"I don't know. I used to be pretty good at carpentry." He angled his gaze upward then back down at her. "And this cabin could probably use a new roof."

She was laughing as he kissed her, and the fireworks began anew...

CHAPTER 5

The morning was glorious. Evie opened her eyes to find that the night before hadn't been a dream. Ray was in bed with her, breathing deeply, still fast asleep. In the bright morning sunshine coming through the windows, she could see the harsh crags in his skin, the dark circles under his eyes. If he'd been human, she would have said he looked really rough.

For an eternally young, near-immortal fey warrior, he looked just plain awful. At death's door. So magically drained that he barely even registered on her senses as having any magic at all. She could've wept for how close he'd come to dying in that fey prison, drained of magic and life. At the same time, she wanted to hug her son and new daughter-in-law close and thank them over and over for bringing Ray back to the mortal realm.

Realizing the best thing for him right now was probably sleep, Evie left the bed as quietly as she could and started preparing for the day. She checked the status of the battery on her cell phone and headed out into the crisp morning air to give Josh a call.

"Mom! How are you guys doing out there?" Josh sounded happy this morning. As well he should be. He was newly mated, and his father was back in the mortal realm.

"Ray's still sleeping. Honey, I think you got to him just in

36

time. He's at a low ebb of energy, and I think resting is going to be his first order of business for a while yet." Evie walked around the cabin, checking on things while she spoke to her son. Everything looked in order, but the air smelled of snow. *Lots* of snow.

"Do you think you'll be able to make it back here before the holidays?" Josh asked.

The original plan had been to spend the Solstice celebrating Josh and Deena's mating. Deena's grandmother was coming in to officiate over their wedding ceremony, and then, there was going to be a big party on the farm. Deena's family was scheduled to start arriving in the next few days.

They'd been kind enough to give Evie a few days alone with the couple to get to know her new daughter-in-law, but the rest of the next few weeks was supposed to have been spent on the farm, among Deena's extended family. Evie had committed to staying through New Year's Day with her son and his new mate. She wasn't sure what was going to happen now. Ray's recovery had to be a priority, though she didn't want to miss her only son's wedding.

"I'm not sure," she told him, pausing to look off into the distance, observing the storm clouds heading their way. She still had a few days to work things out. Better to get through the coming storm and see how Ray was doing after that before making any plans. "It's going to snow here. We have plenty of firewood and provisions. You stocked the cabin well. And when Ray's got some of his energy back, he can probably just magically transport us to wherever we want to go. For now, though, we're safe and sound. We should probably just stay here while he recovers." Her voice dropped lower. "Your father's been through a lot."

"Yeah," Josh agreed, his tone also growing solemn. "Judging by the fiery monstrosity that came through on his tail, he wasn't in a good place, Mom."

She had to swallow hard to contain the emotion welling up inside her. She'd suffered without Ray here, but he'd been suffering too. The creature had been sucking his magic, which equated to torture.

"We'll take care of him now, sweetheart. That's what matters. Our love will help him recover. I know you never got a chance to know him…" Evie said, hoping to say the right thing to make her son understand her feelings. Talking about such things hadn't ever been easy for her. "But I think that you'll love him as much as I do once you get a chance—now that you *have* a chance. So much was stolen from all of us when he was trapped in faerie."

"At least we have a chance to recoup some of the time we should have had together now, right, Mom?" Josh's words meant a lot to her. That he wasn't rejecting his father out of hand was a good thing. She knew many others might resent a man who had fathered them and then disappeared. Knowing it hadn't been Ray's fault was a good starting place for all of them to forgive.

But she would never forgive the *Venifucus*—or whoever it was who had laid the trap for her mate. She would find them and rip them to shreds given half a chance, submissive wolf or not. Nobody messed with her mate!

"You're a good man, Joshua." She held back the tears by force of will.

"Do you have enough clothes? I left a lot of my old stuff in the closet, and there should be some winter coats that will fit you both." Her son, the caretaker, was at it again. He'd always been there to help her, and look after her, since he was a little boy. It was the Alpha wolf in him, wanting to keep his Pack safe.

"It'll be okay, Josh. The only thing we might run out of is electricity. I haven't gotten the generator started yet, but I'm not too worried. Even if it doesn't turn over, we have plenty of firewood, and there will be fresh snow soon that I can melt for water if need be." She was already thinking of the things she'd need to do if they couldn't get the old genny going.

"Do me a favor. Go out and try to get it started right now, okay? I'll hold on while you do it."

"Worrywart. I'm already outside and around the back of

the house. Looks like nothing has been disturbed since I was last here. I was going to wait for a bit in case the noise of the engine woke Ray, but I guess you're right. I need to see if it works sooner or later, and it's not that loud. Not the way you insulated everything." Wolves had sensitive ears, and the noise from the generator had been annoying until Josh got to work soundproofing that wall of the cabin and the small shed that housed the machine.

She opened the door to the shed slowly, scraping away the layer of snow that was already high enough to meet the bottom step leading up into the elevated machine shed. They'd have to shovel a bit if they got a lot of snow. It was important to keep the door to the generator shed clear.

Evie let her eyes adjust to the dark interior and realized everything was as pristine as Josh had left it. In the old days, all kinds of rodents would have made their homes in here, but Josh had sealed up the cracks that used to allow access and put in screened vents to allow for plenty of air circulation without letting every insect and snake for miles around inside.

"The fuel gauge is reading full," she told Josh as she inspected everything before trying to start the generator.

"I had the underground tank topped off about four months ago when I tuned up the engine," he told her. "You should have no problems, but give it a whirl, just to make sure."

"Okay. I'm hitting the button now." She did so, pleased with the immediate response as the machine roared to life. Her son took good care of the things that were important. A little glow of pride filled her heart. "Can you hear that?" she shouted into the phone over the engine noise.

"I hear it," Josh shouted back. "Glad it works."

Evie watched the gauges for a moment before satisfying herself that everything was as it should be. Then, she turned and left the shed, closing the door behind her. She looked up at the sky again. It definitely smelled like snow...and something else.

"I'm going to hang up now, sweetie," she told her son. "I

think company from the res is approaching."

"If it's Lone Eagle, tell him I said hello. If it's anyone else, tell them to take a hike. The shotgun is right beside the front door, and the shells are on the little shelf above it. Do me a favor and load it, just to be safe, okay?"

She rounded the corner of the cabin and saw her visitor sitting patiently by the front door. "No worries, Josh. It's just Fred. I'll call you later."

She cut the connection as she walked toward the grizzly bear sitting on his haunches in front of her cabin. She held no fear. This grizzly was a friend. More than that, he was a shifter.

"Hiya, Fred," she said in a happy tone. "I've got a robe you can wear, if you want. My mate is back, and I wouldn't want to scandalize him." She winked at the bear, who seemed to grin back at her.

Evie went into the cabin and grabbed the heavy fleece robe that was one of Josh's from the closet. She glanced over at Ray, who was still asleep in the bed, before going back out to deliver the robe. The grizzly stood on his hind legs and shifted before her eyes, becoming a very tall, very muscular bear of a man—no pun intended—that she'd known for many years.

Fred Lone Eagle was the local shaman from the nearby reservation. That he was a bear was something known only to privileged members of his tribe and a few others. She was one of the lucky few. As a lone wolf in his territory, the shaman bear had come out to meet her when Joshua had been very small. He'd helped her a lot in those early days, just after losing Ray. Fred had been a rock of support for her and her son throughout it all and he was a close and trusted friend.

"I saw your smoke signals last night and thought I'd come out to see who was here," Fred said, his smile reaching his eyes as he glanced pointedly at the chimney that was emitting smoke from her fireplace.

"It's a happy day, my friend. My mate has returned." Evie couldn't contain her joy and wanted to share it with friend.

"Well, where in the blazes has he been all this time?" Fred didn't look quite as happy as she was. He seemed more exasperated, but she realized, that was because he didn't know the whole story yet.

"He never left me on purpose, Fred," she said right away. "He was trapped in faerie all this time, and last night, my son and his new mate broke him free."

"Josh? Where is he?" Fred looked around, scenting the air to no avail.

"He's in Pennsylvania with his mate," Evie explained. "When Ray saw me, he just grabbed me and poofed us here with the last of his magic. He thought I was in danger, and he used the last of his strength to get me away." It was such a romantic gesture, her heart melted all over again just thinking about it.

"Pennsylvania to North Dakota? That's quite a trip to make in an instant." Lone Eagle looked impressed.

"You knew my mate was different, even if I never told you exactly how. He's fey, Fred," she admitted, revealing the secret even her son hadn't known. It had been too painful to talk about, and she'd always worried that Josh's fey blood would make him a target.

She'd been on the verge of telling him about his father when he'd left her several months ago. They'd kept in touch, but she hadn't had the heart to break the news about his long-lost father over the phone. As it was, he'd found out from others, and things had worked out as they were meant to be. She was sure of that.

"Well, that explains a lot," Fred said. He might be barefoot and wearing only a robe, but he was a bear shifter, and it took a lot to make them cold—even in their human form.

"Ray's still sleeping," she told Fred. "There was a creature draining his magic while he was held prisoner in the fey realm." Fred frowned.

"Do you want me to take a look at him?" As shaman, Fred was well versed in both magical and medical treatments.

"Would you?" Evie felt relief. Ray had been sleeping a bit too long for her comfort. "He was okay last night, but I'm afraid he really used the last of his reserves to get us both here." She opened the door and led the shaman into the large cabin, her voice dropping low so as not to disturb the sleeper. "Honestly, he looks worse than I expected in the cold light of day. He was trapped for years, Fred, even if time passes differently in faerie than it does here."

Fred's mouth formed a grim line as he padded silently over to the bed. He held out his hands, palms down, over Ray's recumbent form. Closing his eyes, he chanted under his breath, and even Evie could feel the gentle swirl of Fred's pure magic rise inside the confines of the cabin.

Evie positioned herself on the other side of the bed, close to Ray, where he would see her if he woke. She didn't want him to think he was under renewed attack. But she needn't have worried. Fred's magic—as always—was the gentlest tickle of grizzly fur against her senses. It was kindness itself, and strength wrapped in a fierce power that was as benevolent as it was holy. There was a reason Fred was a shaman. He served the Light, and that came through in his every action, and his every word.

"Welcome, Brother," Fred said as he opened his eyes and looked down at Ray.

CHAPTER 6

Evie realized Ray was awake and looking from her to Fred and back again.

"It's okay. Fred is a friend. He's the local shaman. He just came over to check on us and offered to take a look at you. I was worried." She reached out to cup Ray's stubbled cheek.

Fred let his magic fade and lowered his hands. He had a slight smile on his face that spoke of fondness. He was a good friend, and he seemed to have decided Ray was okay in the time it took for him to assess Ray's magical power levels.

"Your mate is more than you led me to believe, Evie," Fred told her with a playful wink. "Your son and his mate did good work freeing another servant of the Great Spirit from evil. I look forward to working with you, if you stay in the area, Ray." Fred held out his hand in a friendly gesture. Ray sat up, leaning on one elbow and grasped the shaman's hand. "I've known Evie and Josh since he was just a little pup. I'm glad they have you back now."

"It's good to be back," Ray agreed, trying to get up, but Fred stilled him with one hand on his shoulder.

"Whoa, there, friend. You need to rest a bit more and get used to being in our realm for a bit, I think. Your magical energy is at a low point. I gave you a little boost, but it's best if these things come back in a more natural way."

Ray subsided, giving up his attempt to rise. He really did still look tired to Evie's eyes.

"It's going to blizzard out there in an hour or two. I'm just doing my final checks on a few folks who live out in the wilderness, like you, before it hits. Is there anything you need?" Frank addressed his question to Ray and Evie equally.

"Josh restocked a few months ago. We've got plenty of food and fuel. We should be fine for a while," Evie reported. "Is there anyone we should keep an eye out for?"

When Evie and Josh had lived here full-time, they'd often kept a silent watch over far-off neighbors who might need a helping hand. There had been one old woman, in particular, who'd lived way out at the edge of the res, all on her own. Her name had been Martha, and she'd been an artist of some renown. She'd been too stubborn to move closer to the rest of her tribe, but everyone had looked in on her from time to time, including Evie and Josh, nosing around her place after dark in wolf form, to scare off other predators and make sure she was okay.

"Martha's daughter is living out at her place now. She reported the sound of dirt bikes last night, but she couldn't tell where they were exactly. I took a look around but haven't spotted any tracks yet." Fred frowned.

"Kids, you think?" Evie asked, fearing Fred's answer going by the look on his face.

"No. There was a gathering last night to celebrate a marriage, and pretty much everyone who's supposed to be in these parts was accounted for one way or another. If someone was out this way riding dirt bikes, it wasn't anyone we know. The tribe is on alert, but it's a big, empty territory. As you well know."

"We'll be vigilant," Ray said. "I'll try to cast a ward or two before the storm hits.

Fred looked skeptical. "Uh…maybe I can help you with that," he said, no doubt trying to be gentle with his doubts about Ray's magical strength.

Ray smiled and shook his head. "I promise not to draw on

my own energy. I can cast it the old-fashioned way, like human mages do. It just takes more prep and a bit more chanting." Now, Ray was grinning. "It won't deplete me. I promise."

"Well...if you're sure."

"Thanks, Fred," Evie told him as she walked with him toward the door. "Now that I've got the generator running, I'll keep my phone charged. Call me if you need me. You know I'm willing to help if you need it."

Fred leaned down to place a chaste kiss on her forehead. "You're a good woman, Evie. I wish you all the happiness in the world with your mate returned to you. And the same goes. You call me if you need anything. We're all hunkering down, but you know I can be here in a half hour if you need anything, even in a blizzard. Bears are tough."

"So are wolves," she argued playfully.

She felt so much joy in her heart with Ray here. Being able to share him with her closest friends was a treat she'd never expected to enjoy again. The fact that Fred recognized Ray's innate goodness meant a lot to her. She had hoped they would be friends, and all the signs, so far, were positive.

Fred left, and Evie returned the fleece robe to the hook on the back of the bathroom door, where Josh had left it months ago. They didn't throw away cast off clothing in Evie's household. Shifters could go through clothes like nobody's business, especially when they were young and learning how to control the shift. Josh had burst so many seams on heavy denim jeans that she'd started buying him stretchy sweat pants during his teen years. Those, at least, were a little harder to burst when a change happened too swiftly.

These days, though, Josh was a master of control. He only shifted in his clothes when absolutely necessary. When attacked out of the blue, for example. That was how she'd first discovered he was having problems with evil people tracking him. After a while, he couldn't hide the destroyed clothing from her, since she did all the laundry in the household.

45

Regardless, old clothes—what few survived—ended up at the cabin. This way, there was always something clean available if they arrived unexpectedly. Plus, there wasn't a washer or dryer in the cabin, and the nearest one was miles away in the little town near the res. More clean clothes meant less trips to the laundromat, which was always a plus—especially now, when she'd arrived with no car.

"If I didn't know better, I might just be jealous," Ray said, sitting up against the headboard and looking all sexy to her Ray-starved eyes.

"Of Fred?" Evie laughed. "He's sweet and all, but he's a *bear.*" At Ray's blank look, she went on. "Bears are way too laid back. Wolves are more high-strung, in case you haven't noticed. We're all about action. Bears are all about ease—until you piss one off. Then, watch out. He's a good friend, but we'd never work as a couple. Our animals really don't understand one another." She made a face that she hoped conveyed her dismay at even the idea of a wolf and a bear getting together romantically.

She supposed it might work for others. *Weird* others, to be sure. But not for her.

"And he's a shaman?" Ray asked as she sat on the side of the bed, facing him.

She loved being near her mate, now that she finally had the chance again. She might not ever let him out of her sight again. At least not for long.

Evie nodded. "Shaman—with all that innate bear magic of his—and M.D. He looks after folks around here in both the mundane and the magical sense. Few know he's a bear shifter, except maybe the elders in his tribe and a couple of others."

"You're one of the privileged few, then," Ray observed.

Evie shrugged. "Shifters can always spot other shifters, and we were technically in his territory, since Fred was here long before us. It took him a while because...you know...bears. Laid back and all, you see? But he finally got around to checking me and Josh out when Josh was just a few weeks old. Until then, I'd been dealing with one of the elders, but after Josh was born, Fred took over checking on us every month or so. He knew what we were right off, and he welcomed us, which was a relief. Once a bear accepts you, he'll go to the ends of the Earth for you. They're loyal creatures."

"As are wolves, if I remember correctly," Ray said, reaching forward to drag her into his arms. She went willingly, resting her cheek against his shoulder.

"Oh, yeah. I'm loyal to you, lover. Just try and shake me loose. I dare ya." She laughed, looking up at his beloved face. It was so amazing to be able to tease him like this again.

"Never," he spoke it like a vow. "You'll never be rid of me again, Evie. Not as long as I have anything to say about it." He kissed her, then. A kiss of promise and oath. A serious kiss for a serious declaration. When he let her go, he looked deep into her eyes for a long moment. Then, he seemed to remember something. "Speaking of which…" He tried to sit up straighter, jostling her a bit. "Do you have any candles? And salt? And I'll need a knife and some water, as well. Oh, and matches." His brow wrinkled a bit as he seemed to be thinking aloud. "I haven't done this in quite some time. I hope I'm not forgetting anything."

Evie thought she knew what he was driving at. It sounded like he was looking for items he'd need to do magic and cast the ward he and Fred had mentioned. Evie didn't know a lot about spell casting, but she attended rituals when she could and believed strongly in the Mother of All. She would help Ray gather the implements and assist in whatever way she could.

About forty-five minutes later, they had both showered and dressed in clean clothes. Ray fit into his son's cast offs as if they were his own, which wasn't too surprising since both father and son were built on the tall and muscular side. The items Ray needed were gathered in a basket, and they stepped outside the cabin to begin. Ray explained things as he went along, much to Evie's surprise, but she found he was doing things that even she could manage. Little acts of ordinary magic, as he called it, that were both simple and potent.

She followed him around the cabin as he drew a thin line in the snow-covered ground with salt. Luckily, she had a large supply of it to use as ice melt, and Ray claimed the bigger pellets would work just as well as the fine crystals for what he intended.

"Won't it matter that the salt is melting into the snow as soon as you lay it down?" Evie asked, watching him work and following along behind, holding the ten-pound bag of coarse salt.

"Actually, this is better than the dry salt ring. No gaps. And even though you can't see the salt, when it combines with the snow, it's still there. It sinks into the ground this way, providing even stronger protection. It's ideal, really," he went on as they walked the circumference of the circle, making a wide disc with the cabin at its center. "This'll be our first line of defense. I'll know if anything crosses this ring, once I speak the words and key it to myself."

"Is this something anyone can do?" Evie asked, though he'd said it was before they'd started their trek.

"Anyone with even a little bit of magic in their soul," he agreed. "Oh, I see." He looked at her, his eyes widening in recognition. "I'll teach you the words, and you'll be keyed into it too. How's that?" He smiled at her, and she was glad she had such a perceptive mate. "It's good for you to know these things. They can help protect you in strange situations like the one we now find ourselves in."

"Knowledge is never wasted," Evie agreed. "My gran used to say that all the time."

"A wise woman," Ray said with respect.

"She was. I mean, she really was a wise woman. She was a priestess," she clarified.

Ray seemed impressed. "Human?" he asked.

"Yeah, but she played with us kids like she was a wolf at heart. Grandpa James loved her spirit. You could see it in his eyes when he looked at her. And vice versa. They were a great couple."

"It's clear they had a good influence on you," Ray said softly as he continued to spread the salt in a thin line. They were about three quarters of the way around the cabin now.

"They were the best," she agreed. "I miss them still and regret Josh never got to meet them."

"What happened to them?" Ray asked quietly, still working steadily on the salt line as she kept him stocked with fresh handfuls of salt from the bag she carried.

"Territorial dispute. It wiped out a large chunk of my old Pack. They were in disarray, which was why I was the next best thing to a lone wolf when we met."

"Still, I know it was hard for you to break with your Pack to mate with me." Ray's voice was soft with remembered sorrow. "You know I felt terrible about coming between you and your folks."

"They made their choice," Evie told him. "And I've never regretted mine. You are the mate of my heart, Ray. They should have understood that I had to follow my heart."

"I still say there was something wrong with your Pack," Ray insisted, his expression darkening. "They shouldn't have been so against us. I wanted to look into it at the time—"

"I told you to just leave it," she interrupted him. "Better to just let it go and be together. I stand by that decision."

Ray was silent a moment then sighed. "If you really feel that way, you know I'll continue to respect your wishes."

"Good." She handed him another cup of salt from which he was taking handfuls to lay the salt line. "Now, how do we do this spell?"

He let the subject of their shared past go and spent the next few minutes teaching her the rudiments of casting a simple ward. They spoke the words he taught her together, and she felt immense satisfaction when she could actually feel the magical ring snap into place around the cabin. They were firmly inside the ring, as was the cabin, the generator and even the wellhead. So far, so good.

It felt so perfect to have Evie at his side, Ray thought as he spent the better part of an hour teaching her about spell casting. He hadn't done this kind of magic in a long time, but it felt good and right to be using it now, back in the mortal realm, where it was strongest. It also felt important to teach his mate—his sweet, submissive wolf mate—how to protect herself from magical intrusion.

While it was true that shifters had a natural layer of magical protection that was just part of what made them able to shapeshift, it never hurt to learn new things, as Evie had pointed out. Evie's inner wolf, though considered submissive to many of the other wolves of higher dominance in her old Pack, was still fierce and would defend her well in most situations. Still, it was important to Ray that she have other means of protecting herself and her den. The early warning that wards provided were a key part of that.

In the old days when they'd been newly mated, Ray had just set wards without even thinking about it. It felt disgraceful to him now that he'd never even thought of showing Evie how it was done. All the years he'd been gone and she hadn't been able to do the simplest forms of magic to keep her home safe. That was on him. He should've been a better mate. He should've shown her this stuff long ago.

They cast three wards in all, each a little closer to the cabin. The final protections would be placed on the cabin itself, from the inside. It was just starting to snow when they went back inside.

CHAPTER 7

"Fred said we were going to have a blizzard, and I believe him," Evie said, taking off her coat and brushing off the light dusting of snow before she hung it on the hook next to the fireplace. She did the same with Ray's coat, so both jackets would have a chance to dry in case they needed to go outside again. She turned back to Ray with a mischievous grin. "I wonder what we can do to pass the time."

Feeling playful, she prowled closer to her mate, joy in her heart.

"Come here, you," he mock-growled, wrapping one strong arm around her waist and pulling her close. He couldn't growl like a wolf, but that was fine with her. As submissive as her inner beast was, Evie thought it much better to have a non-growly mate with fey sensibilities than the other way around.

That said, he certainly knew how to play like a beast. He nipped her neck, leaving tingling little kisses down her throat as he walked them over to the big overstuffed couch across from the fireplace. He swept her legs out from under her, catching her in his muscled arms as he lay her gently down on the soft cushions. There had been a dustcover over the fleece throw that covered the couch, so it was clean and fluffy, as if no time had passed since they'd last been here together.

They'd spent an entire winter, it seemed, snuggled together

on this couch, looking into the flames of many fires…and kindling fires within themselves…for each other. She was pretty sure some of her most memorable moments spent with her mate had been on this couch—both talking and making love.

Evie was all for making some new memories. Right now, in fact.

She pushed at his shirt, wanting it out of the way, so she could stroke his skin. He had such delightful textures to his body, rough where she was smooth, hard where she was soft. She reveled in the contrasts, knowing this man, of all men, had been made just for her.

She succeeded in pushing up the offending fabric, sliding her hands over his chest, and then, Ray helped by lifting his arms and tugging it the rest of the way off. Good mate. Cooperative mate. She wanted to pet him and praise him for doing what she wanted. Her inner wolf wanted to submit to him and play with him at the same time, a never-ending game of affection between them.

While one part of her mind was aware of the increase in the winds outside and the snow coming down to land almost soundlessly on the roof of the cabin, the majority of her senses were occupied with her mate. His delicious scent. The thoughtful way he accommodated her. The dizzying passion that sprang up between them at the least provocation.

He was undressing her, bit by bit, and she was grateful for it. Each new caress made her want him more. He knew just how to touch her to evoke her most passionate responses. Even after all this time, it was as if their bodies had never been apart, never known the loss of each other. It was all perfect. Just as it had been all those years ago.

"You're so beautiful, Evie. Now and forevermore, you're my mate." His words made her open her eyes. They'd shut without her conscious volition, at some point, but she was watching him now, gauging his mood. He seemed so serious. Almost solemn.

Evie reached out to cup his cheek. "Forever, Ray. You're

my mate. You know what that means to shifters. There is nobody else for me. There never could be."

"I wouldn't have blamed you if you'd been able to find someone else while I was away." The look in his eyes was almost painful to bear. There was a lot of regret there. Something she never wanted to see on her mate's handsome face.

"Never, Ray. I'm not wired like that. Once I found you— my mate—that was it. I don't want anyone else." She tried to reassure him.

"I'm just selfish enough to be happy to hear it, even though I know how hard it was for you. Raising a baby. All on your own. I missed so much, and you were so alone. It's one of the deepest regrets I will carry with me for the rest of my days."

She stroked his hair, wanting to erase that look from his beloved face. To ease the burden in his heart.

"Don't do it, Ray. Don't feel bad. I've been talking to Josh since he found his priestess mate, and we've hashed out a lot of reasons why he and Deena both think that everything happened in an almost preordained way. I couldn't speak of you to Josh, which was why he went off on his own quest for knowledge when his magic manifested all of a sudden. If not for that, he never would have met Deena." She stroked his shoulders, wanting so much to make him understand. "Yes, it was hard while it was happening, but now, I honestly don't think I would change it. Oh, I would have rather had you here with me all those years, of course, but our son didn't turn out too bad, if I say so myself." She grinned. "And I think we're all where we're supposed to be now, even if you did poof me halfway across the country without so much as a by your leave."

There it was. Ray's smile. Granted, it was a small one, but it was still a smile. A little quirk of his lips that told her without words that everything was going to be okay.

"You're too good to me, Evie. You always were." He leaned down to kiss her, and she welcomed him, needing to bind with him in the most elemental way. To reassure them both that all was once again right with their own little world. They were together now. That's all that mattered.

Her hands went to his waistband. She allowed her fingers to do the job of unbuttoning and unzipping the old jeans they'd found in the closet. She'd spent quite a bit of time appreciating the way his butt made a bit of otherwise ordinary, worn denim into something truly drool-worthy.

Hubba hubba. Her man looked good in faded jeans. Josh was never getting this pair of pants back. Never. She was appropriating them for her mate, and that was the end of that.

But right now, the jeans had to go. Evie didn't want anything between herself and her mate. His kisses grew more urgent, and her passions rose. It wasn't quite as explosive, as quickly, as the night before. Thankfully, they'd taken the edge off a little and were able to go at a slightly less frenetic pace this time. But it was still pretty darn combustible. Sparks of golden light were already beginning to form. Just small ones right now, but if last night was anything to go by, there would be fireworks inside the little cabin soon enough.

Ray seemed to get the message about his jeans. His hands took over the job, and within moments, the fabric was gone. Minutes later, the rest of her clothing followed. Finally. They were naked. Together. On the wide couch where they'd spent so many evenings together, so long ago.

It was all new now, though. Even as it felt the same. They were older. Perhaps wiser. Their separation had only made their hearts and bodies yearn more.

Ray stroked her skin with long caresses of his hands. He rubbed his hard body against her softness, positioning her the way they both liked. She was surrounded by him, tucked into the couch, enveloped by warmth from below as well as above. On one side, the couch kept her cozy, and on the other was the roaring fire in the fireplace, not too distant. She was cocooned in warmth…and love.

Only one thing was needed to make this experience

complete. Ray.

He claimed her body slowly, pushing inward carefully. She had been a bit swollen that morning, but her accelerated shifter healing had fixed her before they'd even started their day. Still, she wasn't used to sex anymore. She hadn't had any for the twenty or so years that Ray had been gone. She simply couldn't. Not with anyone but her mate.

Ray's care was appreciated, and as he claimed her, seating himself fully inside of her, she stroked his shoulders and back. He was such a considerate lover, and always had been.

"You okay, sweetheart?" he asked, his breath coming in short pants as he seemed to struggle to keep still.

She squeezed him with her inner muscles, drawing a groan from his lips that made her smile.

"I'm good, but if you don't start moving soon, I'm going to flip you onto the floor and have my wicked way with you."

He grinned. "You promise?"

Evie nodded, holding his gaze.

"I'll keep that in mind for next time. For now, though…" He didn't finish his sentence as he began to move.

After last night, they were even more attuned to each other, and it wasn't long before the bright golden light of their magic sparked off each other. It started to swirl around the cabin, pulsing in the rhythm of their love. Faster and faster it went, reaching higher and higher, right along with Ray's motion and Evie's desire.

It was harder to see, this time, because it was still daylight outside, and the reflective properties of the snow outside their windows made everything seem a little brighter in the small cabin, but the light show was still pretty intense. Evie wondered idly if this was something only she and Ray could see, or if they'd have to practice discretion when out in the world where mortals might notice sparks of magic coming from a particular hotel room or house.

But such thoughts were wiped from her mind when Ray changed position slightly, stealing her breath. The sensations were even more intense, somehow. What she'd thought couldn't get any better, just had, and it was about to blow the top off her head.

"Ray!" she cried in warning a split second before she ignited, her climax hitting her all at once, deep and devastating.

Ray wasn't far behind. He tensed above her, his muscles straining as he found his own fulfillment. They didn't move apart for a long time as the orgasms rolled over them both for long, delicious moments.

Eventually, though, the release wound down, and after a pause to catch her breath, Evie put her earlier plan into motion. She pushed Ray off the couch entirely and onto the soft rug between the couch and the fireplace. He landed on his back, and she followed him down, climbing over him and smiling in triumph when he finally figured out what she was doing.

"I did promise, after all," she told him, placing kisses all up and down his neck and then moving lower.

They spent the rest of the day and most of the night making love, rising only to spend a few minutes eating, putting the cabin to rights and then setting the final ward that would protect the cabin itself. Then, they made love again, this time up against the kitchen counter top.

It had been a wild day. A passionate day. A day of magic and love. A day Evie would never, in a million years, ever forget.

All the while, the snowstorm raged around the little cabin in the middle of nowhere. And the two lovers inside didn't mind at all.

The next morning dawned bright, clear and cold. The snow had stopped sometime during the night, and the sun shone down on a field of unrelieved white when Evie looked out the window. She was making breakfast for her mate, reveling in the ordinary task. She'd missed all the simple things about being mated when he'd been gone. Just making a meal, providing sustenance for someone you loved. It was special. A caring act.

Ray came up behind her as she stood by the kitchen sink, looking out the small window at the snow-covered landscape. She heard him coming, so didn't jump when strong arms wrapped around her waist from behind, pulling her back against his hard-muscled chest. He kissed the side of her neck, and she accommodated him, loving the affectionate side of her fey mate.

Fey may seem icy and cold, but Ray had always been warm and giving with her. She was about to turn in his arms when her shifter hearing picked up the sound of something out of place in the otherwise silent world outside. She stilled, listening hard.

"What is it?" Ray whispered, picking up on her mood and letting her go, though he stayed close.

"Engines," she whispered back, still listening as the sounds grew closer.

"I can't hear it," Ray said after a few moments. She looked over her shoulder at him, raising one eyebrow. He grinned. "Sorry. I know. It's your werewolf superpower. Do you still hear it?"

"If my mate would shut up for a second, I might be able to tell him," she replied, laughing to soften her words.

She was still smiling when she headed for the door to the cabin, cracking it slightly to let in more sound. He followed close behind, but stayed out of her way. Sure enough, the sound was growing closer, ebbing and flowing.

"It's like they're moving in circles, but they're getting closer." She closed her eyes for a moment to try to distinguish more. "Three separate tones. Snowmobiles, I'd say. Nothing else could really get around in this." She opened her eyes and looked toward the buildup of snow against the bottom of the door. There had to be almost three feet drifted against the door to the cabin.

"How much snow did we get overnight?"

"A couple of feet, but as you can see, it's drifted a bit." She pointed to the wedge of snow that had been blown against the bottom of the door.

"I hear it now," Ray whispered, a look of concentration on his handsome features. "No. It's gone. Can you still hear it?"

Evie shook her head. The sound had drifted away and then stopped entirely. "They're gone, I think. Either that, or they stopped their engines for some reason. Either way, they weren't very close. Sound carries over the snow. They were probably miles away."

"Mmm," was Ray's thoughtful response.

He seemed to be mulling over her words as she closed the door on the cold air that had infiltrated their cozy nest. But the fire was still going, and it wouldn't take much to warm the house up again.

"You think maybe they were Fred's dirt bikers, come back on snow-appropriate machinery?" Ray asked after she'd returned to the kitchen area to continue working on breakfast.

"It's a possibility, but there's no way to tell," she replied, frowning as she worked.

"Until something happens," he finished her sentence, and she felt a bit of dread creeping into her thoughts. If he felt it, too, then the feeling of danger in the air might be something real.

"We'll have to be vigilant," she said firmly, nodding as she looked at him. "We're all alone out here, but you set those wards, so that should give us some warning if they *are* bad guys, right?"

CHAPTER 8

Even as she said it, the first ward sounded a warning in Ray's mind.

"What was that?" Evie asked. Of course. She'd helped set the wards yesterday. They were keyed to her, as well. She had to have felt it when the first ward was breached.

"That's what you'll feel when someone goes past any ward you cast," Ray told her.

"So, that means..." Ray hated the look of fear on her face. "Someone just..."

"Entered the first ward," he confirmed.

Panic flared in her eyes. He hated seeing that. Her wolf may be submissive, but it could be fierce when needed. He needed her to tap into that fierceness now. But first...he needed her calm.

"It could be innocent," he offered. "Non-magical humans, at this point, would be feeling uncomfortable, though they wouldn't realize why. The ward would push them back, without any overt action. The farther they walked into the protected zone, the more uncomfortable they'd feel, and most would turn around unless there was some compelling need driving them onward," he said. "If they make it to the second ward, there is reason to be more concerned."

"It'll feel the same?" Evie asked, calming, but clearly still on edge.

Ray nodded. "The breaching of a ward feels pretty much the same, regardless of the size or shape of the ward. The reverberation you felt is just meant to be a warning signal to allow the person who cast the ward to know it has been breached. Once you know what to expect, it shouldn't be as distracting, so if you need to fight, your concentration won't be broken by it."

Evie took a deep breath. "Good to know." She was recovering her equilibrium as he watched, digging into that core of strength he knew she had. Good. That's what he'd hoped for.

Then, the second ward was breached.

Evie went straight to the door and the shotgun hung on the wall next to it. Good girl. She stretched to reach the little shelf above the gun and he felt unaccountably aroused at the sight of her loading shells into the long gun. There was the fierce little wolf he loved.

"If they cross the third ward, they'll be too close to the house," Evie said. "I'm going outside to see what's what."

Ray shook his head. "Too dangerous."

"Not for me. I have some natural protection from magic just by virtue of being a shifter. Plus, I can always go wolf and outrun anything anyone can throw at me."

"Wishful thinking, Evie," he warned.

She turned to face him. "We can't be caught in here like mice in a trap. They could burn this place down with us in it. My wolf says go out in to the open spaces. It's safer."

Ray wanted to argue, but her instincts were probably right. This cabin wasn't exactly fortified in the way he'd like. Stone would've been a better building material, for instance, than wood. But he hadn't been taking magical battles with evil mages intent on killing them into consideration when they'd moved in all those years ago.

"All right. But we'll both go." He reached for his coat even as Evie took off her sweater. "No coat?" He knew her wolf blood kept her warm even in her two-legged guise, but it was well below zero out there.

"Less layers means an easier shift if I need it. And you know I don't feel the cold the way you do. You want the shotgun?" she offered it to him, but he declined.

"Better you keep it and watch my back. I'll take point." She didn't argue, and he was glad she realized this was more likely going to be a magical battle rather than a physical one. Of the two of them, he was the mage, though as a shifter, she did have her own magic...just not quite the same sort.

"If I go wolf, I'll try to get the gun to you before I shift," she agreed, nodding.

He went right up to her and pulled her close for a quick, hard, deep kiss that he hoped said more than he could explain in words at the moment. He loved this woman more than anything in the universe, and facing danger with her at his side was both terrifying and oddly reassuring. There was no one he trusted more, and though he'd rather she was out of danger completely, he knew he could count on her.

He hoped she understood everything he was trying to say but couldn't. For one thing, they didn't have time. Those who had breached the wards were growing ever closer. For another, how could Ray encapsulate, in just a few words, how much having Evie back in his life meant to him? How would he ever be able to explain the depth of his love for her? He didn't think it was possible. Spoken or written communication could not capture the breadth of his emotions when it came to this woman. Words were simply inadequate.

He tried to put it all into the kiss, but there wasn't enough time to do it right. He prayed they would have more time together—as much as the Mother of All would grant them in this life and any future existences they might be blessed enough to share. He drew away, letting her go, though he didn't want to ever let her go completely.

"Stay out of sight. Let me try my hand against them, first, and join in if either it looks like I need help or you think you can do some good without putting yourself in too much jeopardy."

"Ray, I'm a werewolf. A predator. I can definitely help." She rolled her eyes at him, and he found himself grinning. How he loved his spirited mate.

The wolf spirit that shared her soul was fascinating to him, and he loved when Evie followed her instincts as she was doing now.

"Just have a care for my delicate sensibilities," he teased her. "Stay low and let me take the initial barrage, if there is one. Watch and pick your moment. That's all I'm asking."

"Well, of course," she said, exasperation in her tone. "Now, let's get in position before they get too close and we lose all possibility of stealth."

"Were you always this impatient?" His lips curved upward, even as he sent a little tendril of magic out through the small crack he'd made by opening the door less than an inch.

He wanted to scout the situation, as it were, as much as he was able before he stepped out there. The area in front of the cabin was empty. The third ward had not yet been breached, but even so, those approaching seemed to be coming at the place from different directions.

"One coming straight for the front door, but he's too far out to see much of anything unless he has binoculars," Ray told her, closing his eyes to concentrate on what the magic was telling him. "One approaching from either side at forty-five degree angles to the front. They expect us to be inside the cabin, and they're concentrating their firepower toward the only door." He opened his eyes, having learned all he could at the moment.

"Human?" Evie asked as they snuck out the door and closed it behind them. They crouched low, taking cover behind whatever they could find. Mostly that consisted of snow drifts and rocks covered with snow.

"Mages, certainly. Most probably of the human variety."

Evie sniffed the air. "Wind is wrong. I can't smell them yet."

She made a little spot for herself behind what he

remembered as a decorative pile of the striped rocks that made up some of the formations near here. She'd be safe behind the rocks, even though they were covered with a thick layer of snow.

Ray set himself up as the obvious target, not completely visible behind drifted snow and more of the rock displays they'd set up ages ago in front of the cabin. Evie was on his right and close enough that he could keep an eye on her, but she wouldn't be visible, even to the mage who was making from the front right corner of the cabin.

"Keep an eye on the one coming in from your direction. I'll keep the other two occupied," he told her, hoping the mage on the right was one she could handle if things got too hairy for him to deal with them all.

"Just pay attention to what you're doing, Ray. I've got this. Don't worry." Her low voice settled his nerves. She was such a good match for him.

"I love you, Evie."

"I love you too, Ray. Now, give 'em hell, so we can go back to our enjoyable vacation in the snow."

Her words made him smile, and at that moment, the third ward was breached. He could see the middle mage now, walking boldly through the snow toward him, and Ray knew the exact moment when the trespasser saw him. Now, they'd finally find out what these three intended, though Ray suspected it was nothing good.

Ray was about to speak a greeting, though the man was still about fifty yards out. But just then, he saw a fireball rise to life between the man's outstretched hands. *Shit.*

Ray prepared as best he could, hoping the hasty protections they'd put on the cabin would protect the structure. It was clear these visitors had destruction in mind and didn't even want to take time to chat before launching an attack. They weren't really trying to be stealthy anymore. They'd felt the wards.

They'd probably hoped to sneak up on the cabin, which was why they'd come in on foot, but the moment one of them crossed the first ward, they must have realized stealth wasn't going to work. Overwhelming force was the next logical tactic in this case. Hence the frontal assault.

Ray glanced at the two other mages, who he could now see approaching from each corner. Both of them had energy growing between their outstretch palms, as well. All three mages were forming their own versions of fireballs to lob at him—probably all together. The next few minutes would tell the tale of whether or not Ray was strong enough to withstand their combined power, because there was no way he'd dodge and allow any of that to hit Evie directly. Just the peripheral contact was going to be a lot for her to handle.

He wanted to look at her before the volley of hellfire was launched, but he didn't dare. The enemy was concentrating on him. With any luck, they didn't even know she was there. The final ward that was only about ten feet from the structure of the house should keep out any magical probes. Until the mages actually walked across it, the ward would keep out their probes, though it probably wouldn't withstand the hellfire they were about to throw.

It would be soon now. All three had dangerous balls of glowing fire between their palms. Ray took a second to analyze each. The mage on the left was female, and her energy was a dark, sickening gray. Smoke, it looked like, more than fire, but he knew such things were often deceptive. That roiling mass would burn him magically, just as bad as the much larger ball of red between the center mage's hands.

The mage on the right—the one closest to Evie's hiding place—was male, and his fireball was a sickly yellow. It wasn't anything near the sparkling gold of the power that rose when Ray and Evie came together. No, this was from some dark place. It was the yellow of infection. The yellow of evil. And he knew it could burn. He'd come across that disgusting color in battle with evil before.

He'd prevailed then, and he prayed to the Lady he served that he would prevail once more.

There was no time left to think. Everything went into slow

motion as he saw the mages launch their hellfire in a coordinated move, only split seconds apart. Ray reinforced his magical shielding and extended it to cover a diameter that included Evie and the little rock formation she was hiding behind.

When the hellfire hit, Ray staggered, but his shield held. It flared so bright that he couldn't really see for a several long moments, but he was undamaged. He looked at Evie and saw the grim determination on her face as the flare of the shield hid them from the bad guys for a moment. She was unharmed and ready for action, thank the Goddess.

"That answers that question," Ray said, just loud enough for Evie to hear. "They're strong, but if they didn't take us out with that combined blast, we stand a good chance."

CHAPTER 9

Evie took heart from Ray's words, but she knew this battle was a long way from over. She took aim between two of the rocks she hid behind, just waiting for the optimal distance and angle to unload both barrels of the shotgun.

The attackers drew closer, but it was the one in the middle who seemed like the leader. He moved faster than the other two. Evie didn't have an angle on him, but she was waiting for the shot on the male mage closest to her position. He wasn't quite there yet, but in a few moments, she'd have him in her sights.

"You might as well give up now," the leader called out as he walked closer. His steps were very deliberate as he began forming another fireball. "I felt the disturbance when you arrived, but judging by the weakness of the signal, you'll never stand against us. Not for long, anyway."

"Leave now, and I'll let you live," Ray replied. Damn. Evie was proud of his defiance. Her mate was brave, which impressed her wolf all over again.

The mage didn't slow but scoffed as the fireball grew between his hands. It glowed an evil red that hurt Evie's eyes when she dared to glance at it.

"If it weren't for the taste of fey in your energy, you wouldn't even be worth stalking," the man said. "We normally go after bigger prey, but we've already bagged all the shifters we could get out from under the bear's nose." He sneered.

Evie knew he was talking about Fred. Fred was both a bear and a shaman. Great magic flowed through Fred's veins, and he was in a protector role for all those around him. If these three were scared of Fred, they would never be able to harm Ray.

Well…not Ray at full strength…but she didn't know how well his magic had recovered after his ordeal.

Some things started to make sense to Evie. The mages thought Ray was weak. They knew enough to know the flavor of his magic was fey. But did they realize he was a full-blooded fey at low strength when he poofed over to North Dakota? Or did they think he was a part-fey hybrid of low power to begin with?

And was Ray's magic recovered enough now to defeat these three human mages? She wished she knew, but that was something only Ray could know.

Evie steeled herself. She would do everything in her power to help her mate in whatever way he needed. She'd start by blowing a couple of holes in the nearest mage as soon as he…stepped…into…her sights.

Bam!

Evie loosed the fury of the shotgun at her target, taking the man to his shattered knees. The second blast caught him in the shoulder as he dodged, and she regretted the split second that meant the difference between a clean kill shot and this. Now, they'd still have to deal with the guy, once he recovered a bit.

For now, though, he was down. The other two were engaged in magical battle with Ray, a cloud of dark gray and red pounding against Ray's magical shield. Evie was far enough away to scoot out around the edge of the shield, if she chose. She checked the status of the mage she'd shot, and he was flat on the ground. No chance to get him with the shotgun again at the moment, and the other two were surrounded by shields of their own that Ray was assaulting magically.

Mundane buckshot would never make its way through such magical protections, so it wasn't even worth trying. Worst case scenario, anything she shot at those other two would bounce off their shields and come right back at her. That wouldn't be good.

Deciding she couldn't do anything about the other two, right now, she thought about her next move. The shotgun was useless at the moment, so she put it down. The mage she'd shot was still writhing around on the ground. She couldn't shoot him, but her wolf scented his blood and was prodding her to do things the old-fashioned way. The wolf wanted blood.

Stripping quickly, Evie let the shift happen. The wolf burst out of her skin, happy to be free and ready to fight.

She slunk as fast as she could around the edge of Ray's shield and headed out, bounding across the space between herself and the downed mage. There was so much magic flying, the other two didn't even seem to notice her. The one she'd shot, though... He saw her coming, and he tried to lob some of that evil yellow magic at her.

It didn't really work. The lightning he tried to shoot at her dissipated against her fur. It tickled a bit in an unpleasant way, but it didn't hurt her. In fact, it only made her angrier. She moved faster, but the closer she got to her foe, the stronger the ochre lightning bolts became. It started to piss her off, even as the unpleasant tickle became painful.

Little daggers pricking through her fur into her skin in a million places enraged the wolf as it went in for the kill. The mage was sitting up now, bleeding profusely, but using his magic in a way that had him healing before her eyes. The blood seemed to empower him, which she knew was a seriously bad thing.

Blood magic was among the most evil. And, unfortunately, the most powerful weapon the enemy could employ.

Damn. If Evie had felt even one qualm about killing the

man, the fact that he was a blood path mage would have convinced her. He had to be stopped, and she didn't have the luxury of just knocking him out and hoping he didn't pop back up again at an inopportune moment.

No. In this situation, with two others attacking Ray with all their combined power, this third guy was one too many. He had to go down with no possibility of rising again. The wolf wanted to howl. It wanted the kill, and Evie consciously sent her human awareness to the background and let the wolf instinct take over.

She pushed through the pain and closed on her prey. He was wily. Even injured, he still had teeth. Those lightning bolts he was firing hurt like the dickens!

"Dirty shifter scum," he muttered, redoubling his efforts with the lightning. The bolts caught her in the flank, and she bit back a whimper. Sonuva…

Evie stalked closer, using her mind as a weapon. Mind over matter. Thought over pain. Shifter magic rose and allowed the evil lightning to dance off her fur and dissipate into the ground around her as she moved closer a step at a time. It was like walking into a hurricane force wind. The closer she got to the eye of the storm—the mage—the stronger the force that came against her.

But Evie was made of tough stuff. Her wolf was a fighter, and she was protecting her mate. She could do anything. *Anything.* For Ray.

The mage raised his hands one more time, but she was close now. She snarled, reaching out to bite him. She bit straight through his hand, wrenching her head and yanking the mage by the arm. Positioning him just so… His bare neck was within her grasp… And then, she struck.

Ray felt the change in the energies when Evie shifted to her wolf form. He'd seen her down one of the mages with her shotgun, but he knew the guy on the right wasn't dead. The three mages who were arrayed against him had linked their power, though they fought individually. He could feel the sickly yellow power of the guy on the right in the mix as the other two threw their magic at Ray's shield.

Only a few minutes after Evie loped away in her wolf form, Ray felt the yellow mage's energy go. He was dead. The trio was now a duo, and the two remaining enemies staggered a bit as the yellow mage's energy was lost to them.

Good.

Ray wanted to know where Evie was, but there was too much magic flying. His pure golden sparks fought against the roiling red and gray miasma that tried to slip through his shield.

"Give up yet?" Ray called through the fog of the battlefield. He could just make out his opponents some yards distant.

Ray was glad he'd had time to recover after porting them to the cabin. If these three had found him when he'd been so vulnerable, this battle would have turned out much different. As it was, Evie had taken one out of the battle already, and Ray was closer to full strength than he'd believed possible. Being with his mate again had restored him more than he'd expected.

Only the need to defend them had made him explore the depth of his magic, and what he'd found surprised him. The channel that connected his soul to Evie's was pulsing with power. It was going back and forth between them, amplified by their nearness, one strengthening the other as they were strengthened in turn. It was the miracle of true mating. They made each other stronger just by being together.

How he'd missed her while he'd been away. It pained him to think that he'd brought this battle down on their heads by using the porting magic that was so noticeable in this realm. He should've waited to find out what was going on in that stone circle when they'd brought him back, instead of panicking and grabbing Evie to port out here.

He hadn't been in this kind of battle in too long. He'd held up well to this point, but he couldn't let Evie do all the work. It was time Ray called upon the power he'd dared not try yet since being released. He wasn't altogether sure of his welcome, but if ever he needed the approval of the Mother of All, it was now.

Ray looked within himself and prayed to Her for the grace She had promised him when he'd agreed to serve her as a Knight of the Light. A benevolent feeling flowed through him as he felt the familiar sensation of the energy armor She empowered Her Knight to wear materialize around him.

He dropped the shield. He didn't need it anymore. Almost nothing could get to him through the armor, and Evie was out from under the shield already, anyway. If she'd been next to him, he'd have kept it up in order to protect her, but as it was, the very best way to protect his mate was to end this battle quickly.

The fog was clearing as the enemy regrouped. He could see them more clearly now. The red mage facing him squarely in front of the house, the female smoke mage off to Ray's left. Both were watching him closely.

"What are you?" the woman asked, as if she hadn't consciously let the words form. She had a puzzled expression on her face. She'd never seen energy armor before, no doubt. It was a special thing afforded only to the Goddess-sworn *Chevalier*.

The red mage looked grim. If Ray didn't miss his guess, the man had just realized exactly what he faced. He'd bitten off more than he could chew, but he was engaged in the battle now. The only options were to run and be pursued, which wouldn't end well for the red mage, stand and fight, which might give him a small chance of success, or surrender, which Ray saw from the man's expression, he would never do.

Fight, then, seemed to be the order of the day.

Ray reached behind him and unsheathed the double swords of pure golden energy that he wore strapped to his back when he wore the armor of the Lady. Most Knights fought with a single broadsword, but Ray had always favored two curved blades since he was ambidextrous. He'd studied

71

sword work with the great masters of the mortal realm and of faerie before he'd even been asked to serve as a *Chevalier.* With such a background, the Goddess had allowed the small modification to the armor She gave all Her Knights.

The blades were made of energy, but they cut just like the highest-grade steel. They also burned through magic and could repulse magical attack if Ray chose to use them that way. Just drawing them made him feel better. He saw the way the smoke mage's eyes widened as she gulped. The red mage just looked grimmer as Ray stepped forward. He would meet the enemy on open ground, away from the cabin to minimize any potential damage to the structure. Ray and Evie would need someplace to sleep that night, after all.

Ray didn't plan to lose.

CHAPTER 10

Evie hid behind a little pile of rocks. The yellow mage was dead, and his blood was on her fur. The taste of it was human, tinged with evil. Evie spat repeatedly, trying to get it all out of her mouth. Her human side was repelled by it, but her wolf side rejoiced in the clean kill.

After tasting his evil, she felt even more justified in her actions. This man had deserved to die. The blood of too many innocents was on his hands. The echo of it lingered in his own foul blood. Shifters of different types. Many werewolves had fallen to this man, as well as a few others that were harder for her to place.

Evie was laying low, evaluating the situation. She wanted to help Ray, and her wolf was eager to rejoin the battle, but she had to be smart about this. The other two mages had to know something—or someone—else had taken out their friend. She'd exposed the fact that Ray wasn't alone out here.

She had feared, at first, that the remaining mages would concentrate part of their attack on her, but she should have realized that Ray wouldn't allow any such thing. He'd distracted them, doing something that grabbed all their attention.

She glanced over at him and paused. Through the smoke of the battlefield that separated them, she saw an unearthly glow surrounding her lover. A golden sheen that overlay his physical body with…armor. Glowing, golden, magical armor.

If she'd ever doubted his word that he was a chosen Knight of the Mother Goddess—which she hadn't—all doubts would have been removed at the vision before her. No wonder the two mages were completely enthralled. It wasn't every day a Knight of the Light revealed himself in all his glory.

That he did so, now, meant these two evil beings weren't long for this world. The predator in Evie's soul rejoiced in the battle that was about to escalate. The bad guys had kicked a hornet's nest, and they were only just beginning to realize it.

Evie knew neither one of the remaining enemies could be allowed to escape. She didn't think the man would back down from his fight with Ray, but the woman… Evie knew what she had to do. Skirting wide around the field of battle, she prowled behind the two enemy mages, cutting off their escape. If one of them tried to cut and run—and Evie's money was on the woman to try it—then they'd have to face Evie and the very angry she-wolf she had become. How dare these people try to harm her mate? For that alone, her wolf wanted them dead.

Bloodthirsty little thing.

Evie realized in that moment that, while she might've been the most submissive wolf in her old Pack before she left, things had definitely changed. Those intervening years of living hard with only herself to rely on to protect her cub had molded her into something more. She was now a silent, relentless hunter that was fierce in defense of her family.

Evie was stronger than ever, and her level of dominance when it came to the battlefield was completely new. No longer was she the most timid hunter in the Pack. No, she had come into her own, and it was about damned time. These people had done exactly the wrong thing if they expected a pushover submissive wolf.

Threaten her mate, and she became a tiger on the inside, not just a wolf. Metaphorically speaking, of course. She'd never met a tiger shifter herself, but she'd heard they were pretty fierce. Even if they were cats.

The wolf sniffed at her own thoughts and positioned herself behind the female mage. She kept Ray in sight, as well, amazed when he drew twin curved blades of what looked like pure magical energy over his shoulders, from behind his back. As he began to move with them, she realized he *really* knew how to use those weapons. They weren't just for show.

He began a dance of death that mesmerized her as the blades twirled and looped, creating an impenetrable defense that repulsed every mage bolt and fireball the two attackers tried to throw at him. All the while, Ray advanced, getting closer to the enemy. Bringing the fight to them. Giving no quarter. Keeping them so busy, there was no alternative but to stand and fight.

For Ray wasn't just defending with those magical swords of his now. He was also going on the offense. The blades swooped and dove around him, reflecting the blasts the enemy tried to land, but also issuing forth bolts of that pure, golden, sparkling energy that had become so familiar to Evie every time they made love.

Those gentle sparkles had an edge now as he used his inner magic to strike at his attackers, cutting through the smoke mage's shield first then hitting her with a blast of energy that knocked her to the ground several yards closer to Evie's hiding place.

Evie kept an eye on the downed woman. If she was unconscious, great. But if she was faking, or tried to rise to help her compatriot while Ray was vulnerable, the woman would find sharp wolf teeth at her throat. Evie had her covered.

The smoke mage wasn't moving. Evie watched the woman closely, noting only shallow breaths being taken by what had to be an unconscious body. Whatever Ray had hit her with, it had knocked the breath out of her. Good.

Evie split her attention between watching the unconscious woman and stealing glances at the ongoing battle between

Ray and the red mage. The man was totally outclassed, though he was putting up a good fight. Still, Ray made short work of his shields, slicing through them with his energy blades then swooping around so that his blades made a deadly X. The move was fluid, and the follow-through completed the mage's doom as the X scissored closed, separating the evil man's head from his body.

The red mage fell, and Ray stilled, the golden glow around him swirling to stillness as he looked down at the dead creature at his feet. Ray shook his head, an expression of regret crossing his features, and then, he gazed upward, releasing a prayer for the soul of his enemy to the Goddess he served.

As Evie watched, the red magic seeped away, into the earth, dissipating and being reabsorbed. Neither the man, nor the magic he'd gathered in life, would ever hurt anyone again. It was returned to the earth from which it had come, released for all time, purified by the soil and rock through which it flowed.

Ray didn't like killing, but when there was no other choice, he would do what was required of him. Two mages had died for their evil, but another still breathed. The woman had only been knocked out, and she had to be dealt with. The quicker, the better.

Ray walked over to the fallen woman and knelt on one knee to check her over. Evie came to him then, and he spared a moment to be certain his mate fared well.

"Are you all right?" he asked the wolf who rubbed against his side. She was bigger than an ordinary wolf, magical and deadly. And he was so darn proud of her. "You were amazing, my love," he told her, touching her head and stroking the soft fur just behind her ears for a quick moment.

He would have kept on doing just that if the woman on the ground hadn't stirred. She didn't wake fully, but it was clear she was slowly coming out of the stun he'd given her.

"What are we going to do with her?" Ray asked the wolf at

his side.

Evie gave a soft yip and went tearing across the snow toward the front door of the cabin. It was ajar, just enough for her to get in. Evie, in human form, reappeared a few moments later, hastily dressed in jeans and T-shirt, with ankle-high slippers on her feet and a cell phone in her hand.

"Deena might know what to do. They had to deal with some enemy prisoners a while back. Maybe they can give us a little advice. And if that's a bust, I can always call Fred. He might have an idea or two." She was pushing buttons as she spoke, and Ray heard the call ringing as she hit the icon to put the call on speaker.

"Mom? What's up?" a male voice answered. Josh. Their son.

"Sweetheart, is Deena nearby? We have a prisoner we need to do something with. She's a mage. Human. Bad." Evie paused for a moment. "What did you do with the bad guys you captured?"

"Duncan helped us," Josh said immediately. "In fact, he took care of the whole thing, and he's standing right here. I'm pretty sure he heard what you just asked. Do you want to talk to him?"

"Uh…" Evie gazed up at Ray, and he nodded. Duncan had been his friend and brother Knight of old. If anyone in the mortal realm knew what to do with prisoners like this, it was probably Duncan. "Okay. Put him on."

The sound of the phone being passed took only a moment, and then, a new voice came out of the speaker. It was a voice Ray remembered from long ago.

"How can I help?" Duncan asked, his voice just as musical and deep as Ray remembered.

"Dunc, it's Ray," he spoke for the first time, feeling unaccountably emotional, talking to someone he'd thought he'd never see again. Someone he had fought shoulder to shoulder with against evil the last time it had threatened the mortal realm.

"Ray? Sweet Mother of All! I'd heard you were back. And

already battling the enemy. What can I do for you?" As ever, Duncan was always there for a friend in need. It was one of the things Ray liked most about his oldest friend.

"We killed two, caught one. She's unconscious, but not badly injured. I suspect *Venifucus*. They seemed to indicate they'd been trapping shifters out here, probably siphoning off their magic."

"The one I bit tasted of werewolves and blood magic," Evie spoke up. "He killed many shifters of different kinds, but I couldn't differentiate the others, just many, many wolves." Her tone was grim, her words solemn.

"Blood path, then?" Duncan's answer was just as grim.

"Evie's senses confirm that for one. I suspect it of the leader, whom I ended—probably a little too cleanly, now that I hear this news." Ray frowned, angry all over again at the evil bastards that had darkened their door. "I'm not sure about the woman. Her power manifests as a sort of oily dark smoke."

"We've seen that before. Recently. One of those that came against Josh and Deena had a similar manifestation." Duncan paused for a moment. "I'd better come out there. With all the magic that was no doubt flying during your battle, a little more from me porting in probably won't raise any eyebrows."

Ray shrugged, even though Duncan couldn't see him. "You're probably right, brother."

"All right, I'm coming now. I'll use you as my focus. I'm handing the phone back to Josh now. See you in a flash."

Even before Josh could resume speaking, blinding golden light flashed right in front of them. When it cleared, Duncan stood there, grinning like a fool.

"Ray, my brother, I wasn't sure I'd ever see you again in the mortal realm." Duncan seemed a bit choked up, but then again, Ray felt the same way. He stepped forward, sheathing his blades and allowing the armor to dissipate while he got a handle on his emotions.

"I honestly didn't think I would ever be free of that prison, short of death." Ray moved one step closer, and

78

Duncan met him halfway. They hugged as brothers, too long separated, clapping each other on the back as emotion clogged their throats.

After a long moment, they stepped apart. Ray was aware of Evie talking quietly into her phone, which she must have taken off speaker, no doubt filling their son in on what had happened here only minutes ago. He noted that she was also keeping an eye on their prisoner, but the woman on the ground hadn't stirred again to his knowledge.

"I'm glad you're back," Duncan said, his voice still sounding a little rough.

"I'm glad to *be* back," Ray agreed. "But I know I've got a bit of catching up to do. First on my agenda, once I'm able to port again, is to apologize to my son and his mate."

"Don't worry on that score, brother. Josh and Deena know what happened and understand. They don't blame you for protecting your mate. In fact, I think Josh is very glad that your first instinct was to protect his mother. I know he's worried about her being all on her own, now that he's mated."

Ray shook his head. "You know my son better than I do."

Duncan put one hand on Ray's shoulder, offering comfort. "You have time now to remedy that. The Lady has set you the task of teaching your son how to be a Knight. I have started his training, but Josh's magic is something I haven't really seen before. I think you're the only one with the skills and experience to help him harness the wild nature of his power. He needs you, and he's eager to learn."

Duncan's words were music to Ray's ears. He'd been so afraid his son would reject him out of hand after everything that had happened to their sad little family. But now, it looked like they might have another chance. That Ray might have a chance to get to know his son as an adult—as a comrade in arms. It was truly a blessing from above.

The woman on the ground moaned, and Ray knew his time for reunion with his fellow Knight was nearing an end. It would be easier to transport the prisoner if she wasn't kicking and screaming at the time.

"Duncan, this is my mate, Evie," Ray introduced them. "Evie, this is Duncan." Evie had ended the call and put the phone into her pocket. She reached out now to grasp Duncan's hand, offering a polite greeting.

"Thank you for helping Josh and Deena," she said, and her tone told Ray she was already predisposed to like the man considering how helpful he'd been to her son. Good. He was glad his oldest friend and his beloved mate would get along.

"It was my honor," Duncan told her, grinning at her. Ray recognized the devilish expression in his friend's eyes. "I have long wanted to meet the woman who could so ensnare my friend's heart," he told her. "I only regret I was not in the mortal realm when you two met, or when Josh was born, or was growing up. I would have helped you, if I'd been here."

"Were you trapped too?" Evie asked, clearly curious.

"In a manner of speaking. I was being held, but not by the same forces that entrapped Ray. Still, it took a fair bit of magic to break me loose. I only returned recently, in fact. When the Lords mated. It was their priestess mate that broke me out of my prison." His gaze went to the woman on the ground. "But that is a tale for another day."

"Where will you take her?" Evie asked in a low voice as all three of them observed the prisoner.

"A safe place where she can be questioned. She might have information that could help us in our fight against evil. But her fate depends on her heart and her willingness to embrace the Light," Duncan told them. He looked up at Ray and nodded. "I'd better get going before the residual magic of your battle dissipates too much to hide my port." He bent to pick up the unconscious woman as if she weighed nothing at all. When he stood upright again, the woman in his arms, he met Ray's gaze. "I expect to see you soon at your son's new home. We have much to talk about, the three of us."

"As soon as may be," Ray agreed. "Though we have a bit of cleanup to do here first." He glanced pointedly at the mangled bodies and bloody snow in two very obvious spots behind them. The kills had been quick, but the residue was stark and would have to be dealt with before they could leave North Dakota behind.

Duncan nodded once more, in understanding. "It was a pleasure to meet you, Evie. I look forward to furthering our acquaintance under less stressful circumstances."

Evie smiled back, and then, in a cascading flash of light, Duncan and the woman in his arms were gone. He'd ported out, to only-he-knew where.

CHAPTER 11

The minute Duncan was gone, Ray turned to Evie and took her into his arms. She was so glad they'd both made it through the battle unscathed. She could hardly believe what had just happened.

Ray held her as if he would never let her go. She clung to him, as well, so grateful that he was in one piece. One big, muscled, strong and magical piece.

"I'm sorry to have put you in danger once again, my love," Ray whispered near her ear as he held her tight.

"No," she said, feeling her wolf rise up, her time being overly submissive over. She pushed back so she could look up into his eyes. "You have nothing to apologize for. Whatever happens to us, we're in this together. Whatever comes our way. Got that?"

Ray grinned at her. "Got it," he replied smartly. "But we're going to have to work on not getting into these situations in the first place."

"I can get behind that," she agreed, laughing with him.

He kissed her, just once, a promise of things to come, before releasing her. His gaze went to the red splotches in the snow and the bodies lying inert there, and he sighed.

"I guess we should start by figuring out where these two came from. They had to have had snowmobiles, right? So, they must have parked them someplace outside the first ward." He seemed to be thinking out loud, his expression troubled, as if he wasn't sure how or where to start.

She placed one palm on his chest, drawing his attention. "Leave it to me. Wolves are good trackers."

Evie had already noticed the trail of footprints in the snow from where she had hidden behind the enemy. It would be a simple matter to follow those footprints back to the source. In this case, back to where the snowmobiles were parked.

Sure enough, after a few minutes of walking, they came upon a row of shiny new, top-of-the-line snowmobiles. The keys were still in the ignitions, since there was no one around for miles in any direction.

"These will have to be hidden somewhere," Ray observed. "Do you think your friend Fred might help?"

"I'll give him a call." Evie pulled out her phone and started dialing. Fred picked up on the second ring.

Though Fred seemed surprised by what Evie told him, he was more than willing to help and agreed to come right out and meet them at the snowmobiles. Evie was able to give him directions of a sort, using rock formations and other landmarks to help guide him to the general area. After that, he'd easily spot them in the open terrain.

Ray had been tinkering with the machines while she'd been on the phone. "Fred's on his way. He'll be here in about ten minutes. Luckily, he was already on this side of the res."

"Good," Ray replied in a somewhat absent tone.

She recognized that particular tone from her son, when he was fascinated by some machine or other. Apparently, the apple didn't fall far from the tree. Josh had been motorcycle mad for a number of years, and he'd worn that same expression on his face when contemplating the inner workings of his Harley.

Evie was still a little on edge after the battle. Fighting people lobbing around evil magic wasn't something she did every day. The activity of tracking their trail to the snowmobiles had helped her wind down a bit, but she needed more activity before she would be able to truly regain her normal calm.

Her inner wolf was smugly satisfied at the result of the day's work. It saw things in black and white, good and evil. It was proud to have been part of ending a being of evil, though Evie's human conscience twinged a bit at the idea that she'd killed a man today. She'd never killed a human before, though she knew in her heart there had been no other way.

She'd been defending her home and her mate. Defending one's territory and especially one's mate was paramount in her world. She hadn't really known she'd had it in her until it had happened, and she wasn't exactly sure how she felt about it all. No doubt, it would take some time to sort out her feelings on what had happened today.

For now, though, she was content to be with her mate. Both safe. Both sound. Both living and able to fight another day. That was something. A definite score for the good guys.

Ray must've sensed the turmoil of her thoughts because he gave up his minute inspection of the snowmobiles to come over and wrap his arms around her. How she needed his touch! She snuggled into his warm embrace, inhaling his delicious scent and reveling in the love she could feel in his every touch.

"Tough morning, eh?" he murmured, just holding her close.

"You can say that again."

They stood there, hugging, for long minutes, saying nothing more. It was enough to just be together.

When Fred arrived a short time later, they were still standing there, in each other's arms. They broke apart as Fred approached. He was in grizzly bear form, holding a canvas knapsack in his teeth, of all things.

"Looks like he came prepared," Evie said with a chuckle.

Sometimes, being naked after a shift was really inconvenient, and in populated areas, a supposedly *wild* animal couldn't really carry a purse with all the necessities, though Evie had often wished she could. Out here, though…in the middle of nowhere…she supposed a giant bear like Fred could do whatever the hell he damned well pleased, and there would be nobody to say anything about it.

"I haven't seen a bear that large in many years," Ray commented, watching Fred approach on massive, lethally clawed paws. The snow wasn't giving him too much trouble since it was relatively thin in spots, where the wind had swept it into drifts and valleys.

"You've known other bear shifters?" Evie asked, looking up at her mate.

It always surprised her when he talked about things that had happened decades or even centuries before she'd been born. Mating with an immortal fey was a bit of a mind-bender at times. It could also lead to tragedy—for him, most likely—but the heart knew only love, and the mating would not be denied. No matter what heartache might come down the road.

"I fought alongside shifters and bloodletters in the battle against the Destroyer. I knew many of your kind, once upon a time." He tapped her nose with his forefinger, his mood lighter than she'd expected for such serious words.

Ray let her go and walked forward to meet the bear who was almost upon them. He held up one hand, palm outward in greeting. Fred came to a stop in front of Ray, nodded his shaggy head once, then dropped the knapsack on the ground. He set off slowly, nose to the ground, scouting the area around the snowmobiles in minute detail for a few minutes before returning to where he'd dropped his bag.

His shift was a rainbow of magical dust motes, swirling around his bear form in a blinding light show. Evie had never seen any other shifter give off quite that effect, which had to mean something about Fred's particular brand of magic and level of power. She thought it probably had something to do with the fact that he was a shaman. He'd sworn his life to the Light and to helping people. And bears were reputed to be among the most magically gifted of all shifters.

One minute, the massive bear was standing there on all

fours. The next, Fred was straightening to his full human height, naked as the day he was born. Nakedness didn't much bother shifters. Even in human form, they had some natural protection from the elements. The spirit of their animals kept them warm in situations where regular folk would have been freezing. Still, there was a lot of snow on the ground, and a chill wind blowing.

Plus, if they were going to be driving these snowmobiles anywhere, it was probably best done wearing pants, at the very least. Fred didn't say anything at first, just retrieved a pair of well-worn jeans from his pack, and put them on. He nodded at Ray again.

"Glad to see you both in one piece. I felt an echo of the magic that must have been flying around you earlier, and it was pretty intense," Fred revealed.

Ray nodded. "The battle took place within the perimeter of the outermost and center wards. That probably kept the majority of it contained, but I thought there might be some leakage, considering how hastily we put up those circles."

"Not to worry," Fred told them. "You may have noticed, there aren't all that many people around here, and even fewer with magic of their own. I have my suspicions about those you fought today. I've believed, for some time now, that there was a mage—or perhaps a team of them—watching my territory. Too many of the people who should have been under my protection have gone missing or just left, leaving no word of where they were going. You may just have solved a big problem for me and the Others that live around here."

Evie stepped forward. "The one I killed tasted of shifter magic. Many wolves. Others I couldn't place."

Fred's expression darkened. "Was that the leader?"

"No." Evie shook her head. "Ray took care of him. And one survived, already transported by an ally, to be questioned by the Lords and their people."

Fred rocked back on his heels. "You two work fast. I'm impressed."

"I can't say for certain whether the red mage was preying

on shifters, but he was definitely siphoning power from somewhere—or someone else. After we deal with the cleanup, we can try to backtrack the magical trail and see what we find," Ray promised.

Fred nodded. "Sounds like a good plan. For now, I'd like to see the bodies first, before we do anything else."

Ray agreed, and they each took a snowmobile.

"Ever driven one of these things before?" Evie asked her mate, who was looking both enthusiastic, and a tad apprehensive as he straddled the big machine.

"No, but there's a first time for everything, and I'm usually a quick study. Just…don't drive too close to me until I get the hang of this thing." He gave a chuckle as he started the engine and the machine roared to life.

He was off a split second later, going a little too fast at first, but doing a big loop around Evie and Fred while learning the controls. Evie had to smile. Her mate was, indeed, a quick study and a man whose talents seemed to be endless. She started her own snowmobile, as did Fred, and they set off together—loosely spaced across the wide-open landscape.

Ray kept thinking one thought as they rode across the snow field.

I have got to get me one of these machines.

The moment of enjoyment was unexpected after the rigors of the morning. There was no doubt about it. It felt good to be alive.

All too soon, the joy of this new experience was overshadowed by the memory of the battle that had come before, and the grisly after effects. Evie led them to her kill. Ray didn't care what order they did this in, and in a way, it was probably better to get Evie's part over with first. Perhaps that would help her put it behind her as quickly as possible. He'd have to sit her down later and try to get her to talk about her feelings. To his knowledge, she'd never had to kill a person before, and he didn't want her to be traumatized by the day's events.

He had to help her through it—if she needed it. He had to get her to understand that she'd had no other choice. And in this particular case, the only way forward had been to defeat the evil that faced them. She had done a good thing, but a woman like her, with a gentle heart and strong conscience, might have trouble getting to that place. He had to be her guide and her friend, in addition to being her lover. He would do anything for Evie, and it was important to him that this morning's events not cause her any further pain.

The scene, when he finally got a close look at it, was both gruesome and impressive. She'd executed a clean kill. Her wolf had done excellent work, and it was clear to Ray that the mage had not suffered unduly. That sort of thing would be important for Evie to realize if she had trouble with her actions later.

There was a lot of blood, though. A *lot* of blood. More than any one person should have had, which made Ray's hackles rise.

"I've seen this before," he said, his voice grim in the cold air. "Blood path mages die like this," he told them.

"Then, it is as I feared," Fred said, bending down just outside the wide pool of bloody slush around the body. "This man, at least, was preying on shifters."

"Definitely shifters," Evie agreed. "But there were other magical varieties, too, that I didn't recognize. He might easily have been preying on his fellow mages, or Others of different species. Is there any way you can tell, Fred?" she asked the shaman.

Ray tried to think of a way to get the answer that she sought, but there was no easy spell that he knew to identify traces of magic stolen from their rightful owners, so he stayed silent.

"I'll have a think about it," Fred promised. "For now, we can take the body away, but the blood..." He trailed off, seeming to think as he examined the blood-stained snow.

This one, Ray could answer. "I can purify it and send it to

earth," Ray told the shaman.

Ray was revealing something about his loyalties and his calling to Fred, but he didn't think he was in any danger from the shaman. Fred's purity of heart shone in his every move, his every breath. And the rainbow shift they'd witnessed only emphasized to Ray the true level of Fred's commitment to the Light. Still, it was a big step for Ray, trusting someone he'd really only just met with even a tiny hint of his true allegiance.

Fred seemed to realize what Ray was saying. He met Ray's gaze and spent a moment studying what he saw.

"It would take some time for me to prepare a ceremonial space to do what you suggest," the bear shifter finally said.

Ray nodded, acknowledging Fred's unspoken suspicions. "I can do it here and now. Once we move the bodies, I'll do it fast, before we leave here, and before the magical disturbance in the area completely settles. That way, if these three had friends who might be watching for such things, it won't be as easily noticed."

"That's why you had the survivor transported so quickly, eh?" Fred asked, a sly smile coming to his face.

Ray shrugged. "An opportunity arose. I simply took advantage of it." He wasn't about to discuss Duncan's involvement. Some things would just have to be a mystery.

"I'll take this one on my snowmobile," Ray volunteered. He'd fought the red mage himself and already knew all he wanted to know about the man he'd killed. Fred could take that one on his machine, leaving Evie free to ride alone. Ray could protect her that much, at least.

But when Ray moved closer to lift the body off the ground, Fred stopped him. "Just a moment," the shaman cautioned. "What's that on his wrist?"

Ray looked, but he didn't see… Wait a minute…

Evie stepped closer, looking over Ray's shoulder. "I don't see anything."

Fred made a sign of protection then lifted the yellow mage's arm, turning it over. And there was something there.

Ray's magical vision had never been his strong point, but he could detect the presence of hidden symbols, even if he couldn't see them perfectly.

"*Venifucus*," Fred spat. The ancient word hung in the air around them for long beats of their hearts. "This is worse than I thought."

CHAPTER 12

After that, they checked the other mage's body, and sure enough, he had *Venifucus* markings too. The *Venifucus* were an ancient brotherhood of those who supported Elspeth, the Destroyer, and fought on the side of evil against the forces of Light. Until recently, it had been believed that the order had been wiped out in the last big battle, centuries ago, that had resulted in Elspeth's banishment to the farthest realms.

More recently, it had been discovered that the order had not died out. In fact, they'd gone underground and were actively working to return their leader, to the mortal realm. They'd been gathering strength, and new followers, in secret all this time. They'd hunted and killed those who would have opposed them if the battle had been out in the open. They'd stolen magic from Others who would never have approved their power being used for evil. They'd done terrible things, all with the same goal—bringing Elspeth back.

There were rumors that they'd already succeeded, but nobody had any real proof. If Elspeth was already back in the mortal realm, she hadn't shown herself yet. At least not to anyone who would mount a defense against her evil. No, if she was here, she was being stealthy about it, biding her time, building her strength for what could be a devastating strike.

It was one of Ray's primary duties to fight evil wherever

he found it. He would also be on the front lines of any battle against Elspeth, should it come to pass, as he'd been before.

"We're going to have to take them someplace special to deal with this," Fred said, interrupting Ray's grim thoughts. "Can you still handle the residue?"

As with the yellow mage, there was an inordinate amount of blood under the red mage's body. More than could be accounted for by his death alone. No, this was the blood of those he'd killed in pursuit of power. This was the blood that had powered his evil. Blood of innocents, for the most part, though he'd probably taken out more than a few of his rivals in his time. Blood path mages weren't known for being nice guys.

"I can," Ray answered Fred's question. "It helps that the majority of those he preyed upon were innocent."

Fred nodded and hefted the yellow mage's body easily, placing it across the back of the snowmobile he'd driven. Neither of the bodies had a single drop of blood left in them—an after-effect when a blood path mage was killed. When one of them died, all the blood they'd taken through evil usually fled their body, taking their own blood with it. That was handy, Ray thought, since they'd have to transport the two bodies to Fred's special place, and it wouldn't do to leave a trail of any kind.

As Fred secured the body to the machine, he nodded grimly at Ray. "Do what you must, my friend, and let me know if I can help in any way."

"Thanks, but I can manage." Ray opened his hands, facing his palms toward the blood slush that had been under the red mage.

He called on the Goddess he served, sanctifying the area with the ritual words. As he spoke, he could feel the Light gathering to banish the remains of the dark. A current of power rushed through him when the blood of the innocents was freed from the small residual hold the red mage had on those he'd killed, even though he was no more.

Ray felt it when the last of the red mage's power

disintegrated. Breaking that final bond allowed the blood to dissipate, melting into the ground, leaving no trace behind. A bare spot on the earth was left when all the blood had gone, the deep brown of the soil unmarred by red. And then, a sudden wind rose, and snow drifted to cover the spot, obliterating all evidence of the red mage's passage. Not only the place in which he'd died was covered, but Ray knew all traces—footprints and even his snowmobile tracks—disappeared thanks to the Goddess's blessing.

No one would know the red mage had passed this way. Should his allies come looking for him, they would find no trace. Ray nodded when it was done then walked back toward the place where the yellow mage had fallen to Evie's claws and teeth. He did the same, erasing the yellow mage's passage.

The smoke mage was a slightly different case, since she was still alive, but the Goddess was benevolent, and She gave Ray the power and skill to erase the third mage's presence completely. The paths all three of the mages had taken could not be followed by anyone now. Nobody would link those three to Evie's cabin, which was a relief to Ray's mind. He'd protected his mate and hopefully confounded the servants of evil in the process. As humans would say, it was a win-win scenario.

When Ray returned to where they'd parked the snowmobiles, Evie was subdued, but her strength of spirit was not in doubt. She reached for his hand, squeezing his fingers in silent support.

Fred looked at him with a sort of respectful suspicion as Ray mounted his snowmobile, already laden with the yellow mage's body. They would have to ride a bit slower and more carefully on this journey than they had coming here, but the sooner they properly disposed of the evidence, the better.

"You are a very interesting fellow, Sir Fey," Fred said, one eyebrow raised as he started his snowmobile. "One day, you and I are going to have to sit down for a very long talk."

Ray shrugged. "Perhaps," was the only thing he said in

reply.

It would be up to the Goddess whether or not this bear shifter shaman was made part of the ever-widening circle of those who knew the extent of Ray's service to Her. Though he suspected the time was coming when he and his brother Knights would have to reveal themselves in order to fight the evil he feared was fast approaching, Ray thought the shaman might just be a very powerful ally in that fight, should it come to pass.

Evie was surprised when she saw where Fred was leading them. She'd thought she'd known every square inch of territory around here, but this place was new to her...but ancient in its structure and purpose.

Entering a hidden canyon she had never noticed before, they took the snowmobiles up a gentle incline, crisscrossing the grade as it steepened in an unpredictable pattern. Fred didn't hesitate. He seemed to know exactly where he was going.

Underneath the solid blanket of snow, Evie knew the rock formations beneath them would be striped with the layers of earth that had been laid down over the millennia. It was a unique feature of this area. Erosion and the unstoppable movement of the earth's crust over eons had caused the entire area to be painted in broad stripes of brown, tan, ochre, yellow, rust and every shade of color between darkest brown to palest cream.

It was breathtaking when not buried under feet of snow. In fact, in the warmer months, hikers were common, if not exactly encouraged by the local tribe that oversaw the land. Still, Evie couldn't blame the people who trekked out here, to the back-of-beyond, to witness one of Mother Nature's most artistic settings.

Photographers, painters and just adventurous day trippers checked in at the ranger station for safety, and so area residents would know who to expect out in the wilderness. Occasionally, they also saw trespassers who didn't necessarily play by the rules, or tell anyone in authority what they were doing or where they planned to be. More than one intrepid soul had tried to hide out here, running from the law or their fellow criminals, but they were always found in the end.

Their circuitous route took Evie and the others to the top of a rocky outcropping that was oddly shaped at its apex. In a small depression—so it could not be seen from below—was an amazing rock formation. Covered in snow on the outside, it looked like a big lump with jagged breaks between craggy rocks that towered over her. But when Fred led them through one of the openings, the vision before her stole her breath.

Outside, it was deep winter. Inside, it was warm. No snow. No dust. No debris of any kind.

The striped marks that were characteristic of the rock formations in the area showed here, on the inside faces of the stone monoliths that formed a perfect ring at the top of the outcropping. A sacred circle of living rock. A Goddess circle.

Fred signaled for them to park the snowmobiles near the center of the ring. As she pulled up a few feet from Ray's ride, she saw the low stone altar that sat at the exact center of the circle. When all the motors fell silent, she stepped off the snowmobile and looked around her in awe.

"I had no idea this place was even here," she breathed, looking up at the beauty of the Mother's creation.

No wind howled here. No snow powder flew up to hit her in the face, as it had the whole ride here. It wasn't exactly tropical inside the circle, but it wasn't the cold of outside, either. It was definitely above freezing and warm compared to the snow beyond. This place was a sanctuary that would shelter someone in trouble, and keep safe those of pure heart.

It was a place of worship and would soon become a place of purification. Evie completed her circuit of the natural stone temple and turned back to her companions in time to see them place the bodies of their enemies on the altar. Fred caught her eye and nodded, standing and moving a step toward her.

"If you'd stayed in the area, I would have shown you this

place eventually," he told her, his tone almost apologetic. "When Josh was old enough."

Evie shook her head, smiling at her old friend. "It's okay. I understand. This is a special place that must be protected. Even I can feel that."

Ray moved to stand beside her, his gaze traveling over the circumference of the circle. "This will be perfect for what we have to do," he said approvingly.

What followed, over the next hour or so, was a very intense ceremony. Fred led the ritual, and Ray assisted, seeming to be perfectly in tune with whatever Fred needed him to do at a particular moment. It was as if they had worked together for years, even though they had only just met. Some things transcended time, Evie supposed. And those who served the Goddess, no matter in what form, shared that unifying force in common.

Evie jumped a bit when the magic started swirling. There was real snow outside the circle, but within the powerful bounds of the stone monoliths, a magical storm was brewing. It was the pale gold of Ray's energy, mixed with the rainbow hues of Fred's. Evie felt her own energy rise to aid the spells they were working and knew they would take only as much of her magic as they needed.

Of course, she was willing to help in whatever way she could. She'd played her part in killing one of the men on the altar. The least she could do was lend her strength to be certain he was laid to rest properly, his magic returned to the earth where it could never harm anyone else ever again.

The spell was mighty, and the magical whirlwind was hard to look at. Evie shut her eyes as the power came to a crescendo, blinding white emerging from the myriad colors as Fred loosed the energy he'd been gathering. It coalesced at the apex of the standing stone, in the exact center, above the altar. Then, it descended with a near-deafening boom that didn't hurt so much as startle Evie.

She jumped again as the crash of power flowed out and down, into the earth. When she dared to open her eyes—first, a crack, then wider as the storm dissipated—she was shocked to see nothing left of the bodies that had lain on the altar. They'd been turned to dust, the ashes of them carried into the earth by the whirlwind of magic for all time.

Wow. Evie had never witnessed anything like it before.

"The Mother of All has blessed our endeavors," Fred intoned, drawing his ritual to a close. "Be at ease, Eve, daughter of Morris and Anita Grey Wolf. Our Lady sees the questions in your heart and offers Her blessings upon you for standing with the Light against evil. You had no other choice. You did only what was right in the Lady's sight."

The last few uneasy qualms Evie had harbored about killing the yellow mage dissipated in the Light issuing from Fred's eyes. He was filled with power not entirely his own, and she wondered again exactly how close a servant of the Goddess her bear friend was. Judging by what she'd just seen, Fred was a lot more than he advertised. Shaman, yes. But his magic had grown by leaps and bounds since the last time she'd seen him all those years ago. He was a whole lot spookier than she remembered, and if she wasn't mated to a consecrated Knight of the Light, she might almost be uneasy around Fred.

As it was, she was beginning to get used to having powerful people nearby. Between Ray, Josh, and the priestess who was her new daughter-in-law...and now Fred. Evie felt totally outclassed by the levels of power all around her, and a more insecure werewolf might get a complex of some kind.

Not that Ray would ever let her feel inferior. Not for one moment would he allow that. She knew where she stood with him. They were partners. Not exactly equal in all ways, but they evened each other out. She was good at some things and he was good at others. They complemented each other perfectly. As it should be with true mates.

When the power left Fred, he staggered, just slightly before he caught himself. His eyes were dull with the loss of the intense energy that had flowed through him. Ray steadied him and led him to the altar. Fred leaned against it as Ray moved back, keeping a close eye on the bear shifter.

"That was masterfully done," Ray commented. "Now, if you'll allow me, I'm pretty good with mechanical things. It's a particular talent of mine." Ray shrugged a little as if it wasn't much to brag about. "Since I assume we're going to pass these snowmobiles on to someone else, we'll want to be sure there are not latent traces or traps upon them before we let them go."

Fred looked impressed, and Evie was outright surprised. She hadn't even thought such a thing was possible, but magic and spells was Ray's bailiwick. If he said they should check, they should check. And by *they*, she, of course, meant *him*. Him or Fred. Those two were much better at consciously using magic than she was. With her, it was all instinctual—except for the little bit Ray had taught her about casting wards.

"Please," Fred said magnanimously, gesturing toward the vehicles, parked all in a row.

They were spaced out enough that Ray could walk between them and around each completely. He did this, chanting something Evie didn't quite catch and took his time examining every inch of every machine.

Evie leaned against the altar, now just a slab of striped rock empty of magic and any evidence of what had just happened here. She kept a close watch on Fred. He was drained of energy, which wasn't surprising after what she'd just seen. They watched Ray work silently, and a few minutes later, he seemed to finish, leaving the snowmobiles and heading back toward them. He was grinning.

"There wasn't much on the machines. I think they bought them new only a day or two ago and didn't have a lot of time or energy to spend on them. If they'd been older, it would have been worse, but as it is, they're clean and ready for whatever you decide to do with them," Ray said.

"Me? I thought maybe you two would want them," Fred replied. "Or at least two of them."

"Nah," Evie told her old friend, in perfect alignment with

Ray on this subject, though they hadn't talked it over much. "We're not staying. And even if we did, we don't really need snowmobiles, though they are more fun than I'd realized. Your people could use them, can't they? For one thing, if anybody comes looking for them, which I doubt will happen, you can easily say they were abandoned on res land, which they were."

Fred looked thoughtful, scratching his chin for a moment. "My nephew, Bruce, is the tribal sheriff now," he told her, which was news to her. "He can start legal proceedings in our system. The outside world wouldn't have to know, but there'd be a legit human paper trail if anyone did come looking." He looked her straight in the eye and grinned. "I like it."

"Use them for good," Ray agreed. "That's a win for the good guys."

"And with all the snow this year, the tribal police could use another way to get around. They have a snowcat, but that thing is a monster, and it takes a while to get anywhere in it. These things can just zip around, and if a call comes in for help, they can send someone out right away. My nephew Bruce will put them to good use."

Fred was regaining strength as she watched him, and his eyes were beginning to sparkle with life once more. Bear shifters were really amazing beings. So magical. So strong. Evie truly admired Fred, though she didn't really understand him. Her wolf was always a little shocked by the hijinks bears got up to when left to their own devices, and Fred had pulled some unsurpassed feats of hilarity when they'd all been younger.

"Since these machines are going to the res, why don't you two come back with me? I'll feed you a good meal and then get you a ride back to your place. Sound good?" Fred asked, graciously inviting them onto the reservation proper.

CHAPTER 13

Fred's nephew, Bruce Standing Bear, was about Josh's age, Evie reckoned. He was tall, muscular like most bear shifters—she could tell from his scent and size that he definitely was a bear under that very civilized sheriff's uniform—and had silky-looking black hair and piercing brown eyes. He was a very serious young man and seemed quite distrustful of Evie and especially Ray, until his uncle cuffed his ear and had a few *words* with him privately.

Nothing made a grown man look more like a child than one of his elders taking him to task. Evie would have giggled if she hadn't wanted to rile the young bear even more. As it was, she felt distinctly uncomfortable until Bruce came back and made a very gracious apology for being so standoffish.

"I'm really sorry, ma'am," he said contritely, though he didn't seem to be all that put out that his uncle had given him what-for. Actually, he was handling his rebuke better than Josh would have in similar circumstances. "Uncle Fred reminded me that not everyone is an enemy, though it seems like it lately."

"Have you had trouble here?" Ray asked, his brows drawing down in concern.

Bruce sighed and ran one hand through his long-ish hair. "The res was quiet for so long, I admit we've been

100

unprepared for the stuff that's been happening lately."

At this point, Fred reentered the conversation, walking into the space between Bruce and Ray. He touched both men's shoulders, connecting them in a visible way. Evie knew shamans were all about symbolism.

"And this is where I admit I had ulterior motives for inviting you back here," Fred said, looking a bit embarrassed himself. "I think you might have just eliminated a major source of our recent problems," he went on, looking pointedly at Ray. "But I want to hear your analysis of the mages you encountered—and I want Bruce to hear it too—so we can be sure we're all on the same page. I didn't want to make too many assumptions."

What followed was a detailed discussion of everything they had noticed about the three mages they'd fought. They talked over a plentiful meal provided by Fred and Bruce, who both seemed to be masters at grilling steaks and took turns working the grill while the conversation ebbed and flowed.

Evie told them her observations from the shifter's point of view, which they both seemed to understand, even when she didn't have exactly the right words to express what she'd felt. Ray seemed to connect more with Fred, since they both knew more about the ways of magic than either Evie or, it seemed, Bruce did. Though, as a bear shifter, Bruce probably had way more magic in him than Evie ever would. Still, he was quite a bit younger than Fred, and not a shaman, so that probably accounted for his comparative lack of knowledge.

Some of the things Fred and Ray were talking about were pretty arcane. She just enjoyed her food and let the boys talk. They were definitely on the same wavelength, so more power to 'em.

"I hear Josh is newly mated," Bruce said quietly to Evie while the other two men discussed some minute point of magic. Evie was surprised.

"You know my son?" she asked, perhaps a bit ungraciously. She blushed a bit, but Bruce didn't appear to take offense at her abrupt question.

"I remember him from when we were both really little. You used to bring him with you to the res clinic, right? My mother was the nurse. Still is, in fact. A few times, you left Josh in the daycare attached to the clinic, and we played together. I remember him as a nice kid with a powerful flavor of magic that I'd never felt before...until now." He looked pointedly at Ray. "I see where Josh got that from now. Your mate is something special."

"You can say that again," she said, not really guarding her words.

Had she sounded too mushy? By shifter standards, she was in the prime of her life. She could easily live two or three human lifespans, but compared to Josh and Bruce, she was probably an old lady. She felt compelled to explain.

"We were separated for a very long time. In fact, he's only just been released from the fey realm and returned here. He didn't even know about Josh."

Bruce's eyes narrowed. "That's really rough. I remember you as a single parent, but I didn't know why. I'm glad you two seem to have had a happy reunion, though I guess it's been a bit more adventurous than you bargained for, eh?" His smile softened his words, and she realized he was teasing her.

Bears were quixotic like that. One moment deadly serious, the next joking around.

"It's been pretty wild," she agreed. "I'm just glad we were up to the challenge, and if we've taken out some of your troublemakers along the way, so much the better, right?"

Bruce grinned. "Definitely. We've been harassed by magical traps for months, and several of our shifters have gone missing." His mood changed again, darkening as he mentioned his lost people. "I suppose we know what happened to them now."

"Can I make a suggestion?" Evie asked politely, not sure she wanted to step on this bear's toes in any way when his face wore that dark expression.

He looked at her, one eyebrow raised. "Fire away," he invited.

"If you can backtrack the snowmobiles—or maybe get the identities of the mages from that woman we sent to the Lords for questioning—then you can backtrack to their lairs. If any of your missing people are still alive, you might find them. If not, you might at least find their remains so you can return them to their families and give them a proper send off."

Bruce looked at her with respect in his eyes. "I'll definitely do that. Our tribe is pretty spread out and mostly human, but there are a few of us shifters interspersed in the territory. All the missing were from shifter families. It would be good to give their loved ones closure with definite news of their fates. Or, if anyone is still alive, by some miracle, we'll want to get to them as soon as possible." She could see him thinking as he spoke. "I'd better make a few phone calls right away." He stood abruptly, grabbing for his jacket. "Please excuse me, Uncle." He nodded to Fred and then to Ray. "Sir. Your mate has just given me an idea I have to follow up on right away." He tossed a set of keys to Fred, who snatched them unerringly right out of the air. "Milo can drive them back. Just give him the keys to the tractor."

Bruce leaned down and gave Evie a quick, surprising hug and a peck on the cheek. "Thank you," he told her. "You've given me something I can do to possibly help, which pleases my bear no end. You might even have helped me save a life or two."

"I sincerely hope so. Go get 'em," she told him, feeling the same sort of motherly affection for Bruce she felt toward her own son, even if this big guy was a bear and not a half-fey wolf.

Ray and Evie left the res sometime later in the company of a quiet man named Milo, who was introduced by Fred as another nephew. They piled into a behemoth of a machine with the words Snow Trac emblazoned along the side. It was an older vintage vehicle with tracks instead of tires, but it looked like they kept it in excellent repair. The engine was noisy, so conversation was limited, but Ray managed to figure out that Milo was one of Bruce's brothers.

In all likelihood, that meant mild-mannered Milo was also a bear shifter. The trip took much longer in the vintage snowcat tractor than it had on the brand-new snowmobiles, but Ray didn't really mind. He sat with his arm around Evie as the sky just started to show the first signs of night coming in. They'd had a long event-filled day. He was looking forward to a quiet night at the cabin, free of trouble, to just *be*, with his mate.

Milo dropped them off at the cabin with a cheerful wave. He didn't stop to chat, because night was beginning to fall in earnest, and he had a long way to go before he got back home. Better to take advantage of what light was left while he could.

"Do we have to do anything else tonight?" Evie asked, sounding exhausted as they walked into the cabin.

"Not a thing," Ray told her, though privately, he wanted to do a little reinforcing of the spells they'd cast around the perimeter, just to be safe.

The outer wards had fallen to the trio of evil bad guys, but the protections nearest the cabin were still there. They hadn't been breached, and with the main threat—or what Ray and everyone else sincerely *hoped* had been the main threat—out of the way, that should be adequate for one snow-bound night, at least.

Ray had taken stock of his own personal power during the comparative idle of their dinner with Fred and his nephew. Between donning his armor—which always energized him with the Lady's blessed Light—and just being with his mate, which was a healing balm for his soul, he was regaining strength quickly. He would probably be able to port them out of trouble should anything happen in the night.

In fact, he decided he was going to broach the subject of returning to face the music with Josh the next morning. It would be safer for all concerned if Ray ported himself and Evie while the magical currents in this area were still roiling from the battle. Within the next twenty-four hours would be safest for those they would leave behind here in North Dakota. Ray thought porting into the sacred circle he'd glimpsed in his short time in Pennsylvania would be safest.

The stone circle would likely hide the energy surge from anyone who might be looking for such things on that end. But the sooner they did this, the better. Once the energies had time to settle in both places, the more disturbance his port would make, and the more noticeable on the magical plane for those who might be watching.

Evie sank onto the couch in front of the cold fireplace. Ray went over and laid new logs, using a little zap of his magic to start a roaring blaze. Evie's eyes widened.

"I forgot about your fiery nature," she told him, an inviting smile on her face. "I used to love when you did stuff like that when we were first together. It always reminded me of how special you are."

Unable to resist her smile, Ray sat next to her, tucking her into his arms as they faced the fire. He snuggled her back against his front, enfolding her in his embrace, feeling protective and blessed.

"That was a close one today," he whispered, still dealing with the emotional fallout from the battle. He was a warrior used to fighting, but he usually didn't have his mate—his *mate*, for heaven's sake—in danger right along with him.

And she'd fought at his side. Valiantly. Brilliantly. She'd taken out one of the threats, easing his burden and making the fight that much easier for both of them.

"We made a great team," she said, taking the thoughts right out of his head.

"We always have. I just…" How did he explain the caveman he'd discovered inside him that wanted to keep her hidden from anything that might possibly harm her? He blew out a breath. She knew him. She loved him, for goodness sake. Hopefully, she would understand. "I just regret that we had to be a team in such a dangerous endeavor."

Evie's head tilted to the side in a gesture he knew meant she was considering his words. He was an old-fashioned guy, and he knew the way he talked—a skill he'd learned centuries ago, after all—confused modern people. He tried to keep up with the times, but he hadn't been in the mortal realm in two decades.

"I understand," she said softly, surprising him. He'd expected her to get angry. "Protecting your mate is a basic instinct for shifters too. I can see why having me fighting at your side would make you uncomfortable. But even my wolf knows that, sometimes, the entire Pack has to fight to defend their territory." She shrugged. "It must be harder for you, with no animal to give you such instincts."

He squeezed her for a moment, relieved that she wasn't taking him to task for what he'd admitted. "It's not that I don't want you at my side—my partner in all things—but more that, I didn't want you in danger. You could have been killed, Evie." That last came out as a pained whisper, which had her turning in his arms so she could meet his gaze.

"So could you," she reminded him.

He could see the dampness in her pretty eyes, and it struck his heart. So much had been on the line that day. Both their lives. The safety of the tribe and the shifters it harbored on the res. And more. Those mages had been *Venifucus*, after all.

"But we're okay," he reminded her. "We made it through alive, and our enemies have fallen beneath our blades."

"Well…" She shrugged one shoulder. "My claws and teeth, actually, but those blades you carry are pretty awesome too."

He loved that she could tease him at a moment like this. A moment when emotion bubbled too close to the surface to be pushed down. He wasn't normally a man to walk around with his heart on his sleeve, and it made him uncomfortable, but with Evie, he could show his vulnerable side and rest secure in the knowledge that she would never think less of him. Never use his vulnerability against him. Never make him feel small because he had feelings, hopes, dreams and fears, just like the next man.

Fey weren't invincible, no matter how much some of their

kind had tried to make it appear so. In the old days, when fey played among humans in the mortal realm more often, some had tried to set themselves up as gods or demigods in the form of great wizards and wise men. Some had done it for what they perceived as doing good for the human race. Merlin had been one of those. But some had just been playing, lording it over what they thought of as lesser beings.

It had been easier to travel between realms back then. The magic contained in the mortal realm had been easier to access and had allowed gates to remain open between here and faerie. A lot had changed with the rise of man and the technology the human race had mastered in the intervening centuries. Gates closed and stayed that way. The energy it took to cross the barrier between the realms had increased to the point that only great magic could open the way now, unless you were at one of the few very special points left on the earth where the veil between the worlds was thinner than in other places.

The fact that Josh and Deena had been able to not only break through into the fey realm, but free Ray from the trap he'd been caught in was significant. It meant that Josh and his mate were powers to be reckoned with when they used their magic together. Ray had found out today that he and Evie had something similar when they worked together. Their skills complemented each other's, and they definitely, as she'd said, made a damned good team.

"I took grief from some of my fellows for wanting the twin blades, but the Goddess is kind. She let me fight with the blades I was accustomed to. I spent a great deal of time in the east when I roamed the mortal realm centuries ago, learning their fighting styles. The twin blades were always a favorite, even if they are a bit showy."

She kissed his cheek. "I like you when you're showing off," she told him in a quiet whisper that spoke of intimate moments to come. He rubbed her shoulders when she moved back. "Wolves preen for their mates. I like it when you do it. Don't let what the other guys say make you uncomfortable.

You proved you fight *really* well with those showy blades of yours."

"And you were a magnificent little huntress, my love," he told her. "Your instincts were all that I could have hoped for. You didn't move too soon or too late. You had perfect timing and skills I didn't even realize you had, but probably should have. I mean, you're a wolf, right? I need to factor that into my calculations in the future."

"Oh, there's going to be future battles with us fighting side by side?" Her tone was teasing, but her words brought him back to Earth.

"Yeah." He sighed heavily. "I'm very much afraid there are going to be many battles in our future, though I can pray—selfishly, I know—that you aren't in the thick of most of them. I *am* a Knight and sworn to battle the forces of darkness. I chose that for my life. I knew what I was getting into when I swore allegiance to the Lady. But I never expected to find a mate—or to drag her into the thick of battle at my side."

"Yet, you're battling for the safety of my world, Ray. How can I, in good conscience, not rise to the occasion when everything I know and love is threatened? I mean..." She paused, a look of intense concentration on her lovely face. "I know you're a Knight, and I'd never ask you to forsake that. I know I'm not officially sanctioned, like you, but I'm a shifter, and as such, I protect Mother Earth. All shifters of conscience do the same. It's part of our DNA, I think. We're animals. Part of the land. Part of this earth. It's in our nature to want to protect that against those who would try to destroy it all." She looked deep into his eyes. "Today was different. They were coming after us, in particular, but that was part of the bigger picture, wasn't it? I mean, taking you out and stealing your magic would make them that much stronger in their goal to douse the Light and bring in their eternal darkness, right?"

He leaned in, kissing her forehead. "My smart, eloquent mate," he praised her. "You've got it right. We were fighting for our lives, but we were also fighting for something even more important than ourselves today."

"Then, if more fights come my way, how can I not do my part?" She cuddled into him, snuggling into his arms and laying her head on his shoulder. "My baby is grown and is a Knight like you now. There's nothing—except you, my love—keeping me from helping when and where I can. I mean, I'm not going out to seek danger, but if it comes my way, you can't expect me to sit on the sidelines and let you take the brunt of it. I can help. Like I did today."

"Much as it pains my newly discovered inner caveman, I know you're right. You were a huge help today, and I suspect you will be in the future, though you'll pardon me if I try not to think about that too much. I don't really like the thought of you being in danger. Especially danger I brought to your door, just by my presence."

"Did you ever think that maybe some of it is danger *I* brought to *your* door? I am a highly sought after shifter, after all," she joked, nipping his shoulder playfully.

"The mate of a Knight. The mother of another and mother-in-law of a powerful priestess," Ray considered. "Not to mention your beautiful, powerful, skilled huntress wolf side." He loved the feel of her nestled in his arms. "And your cunning, human, friend-to-powerful-bear-shifters side. Yeah, I can see where you are a truly dangerous woman, and I'm going to have to watch myself around you."

He was joking, but there was truth in his words. With all her connections to powerful beings, Evie was a natural focus of attention should the enemies of Light choose to strike at those around Evie *through* her. Ray decided then and there to do his best to teach her even more ways to defend herself. If she was going to be a target—and he was pretty sure she already was—he was going to make sure she was as equipped as possible to surprise her enemies and get them before they got her. That might help ease his worry. A little.

He kissed her, taking his time. He wasn't sure how long they sat there, the fire warming them from the outside while the kisses they shared lit the heat of desire within. They'd been through so much that day...and since they'd been so cruelly parted.

But they had time now. Time to renew the bonds that had held them together this long and would, given half a chance, bind them together for eternity. Ray didn't know how many years, or even minutes, they would have together, considering she was mortal and he fey. He'd resigned himself to accepting whatever fate allowed them back when he had first met her. His life was not a safe one. He was a warrior by profession, and desire. He fought the worst the world had to offer in the name of all that was good. He had a noble calling, but he was honest enough with himself to understand that his job would probably be the death of him, sooner rather than later.

As such, he'd been resigned to the idea that he might possibly die at any time, leaving Evie on her own. He'd explained that to her all those years ago. He'd just never anticipated that he would be captured and would miss more than twenty years of the short time they might have together. He felt cheated. As it was, even though shifters lived much longer than humans, it wasn't much compared to fey life spans, which were so long as to seem infinite to mere mortals.

Of course, Ray knew he was powerless against the march of time. He resigned himself, once again, to enjoy the here and now and not worry about the future. What would be, would be, regardless of whether he wasted time agonizing over it or not.

That thought firmly in mind, he let time slow to a trickle as he enjoyed the feel of his mate in his arms. She was so warm. So alive. So perfect for him. She always had been.

And she was a living flame in his arms. He'd tried to keep it slow and sensual, but Evie had other ideas. Her writhing movements rubbed him in all the right places, to the point that he had to take things to the next level. And for that, this time, he wanted the bed.

Ray rose from the couch, Evie firmly in his arms. She

giggled as he carried her over to the bed and placed her down upon the quilt. The smile she gave him as he disrobed was one he remembered from the early days of their marriage. Evie had always been able to turn him on with that shy little smile of hers.

When he was naked, he sat on the bed beside her, tracing the curls of her hair that lay over one shoulder with his fingers. Downward from her shoulder, over her arm and then onto the soft swell of her breast, he followed the curl of her long hair, smiling as her breath caught in her throat. He paused at her nipple, circling the peak that became hard even as he watched, poking at the material of her sweater.

The fabric was so soft and the little bud of her nipple so hard. A study in contrasts that made him want to remember this moment for all time.

"Tell me what you want, my love," he whispered to her, holding her gaze even as his fingers played with the taut peak of her breast through the fabric of her top.

"I want…" She was breathing hard as her excitement rose. "Clothes off," she managed the two words, but no more as he rolled her nipple gently between his fingers.

"Yes," he agreed, watching her intently. "My clothes are off." He nodded at the little sound of exasperation that rumbled from her throat. How he liked it when her inner wolf peeked out at him during these playful moments. "Oh, I see. You want your clothes off, is that it?" He pretended he didn't know exactly what she'd meant. When she nodded, growling the tiniest bit, he figured he'd teased her enough. "All right, sweetheart. Let's see about getting rid of some of this fabric, eh?"

He let go of her breast, moving both hands to the hem of her top. He pushed up and managed to get the sweater off in one motion as she did all she could to assist. He returned his fingers to her waist, making short work of the closure on her pants and pushing them down, only to have her kick them away and right off the bed in her impatience. She'd managed to lose the panties, as well, which meant all he had to deal with was the lacy bra peeking at him through the long tendrils of her hair.

Her nipples pushed against the thin lace, and he licked his lips in anticipation. She was eager, but so was he. Eager to get his hands on his mate's luscious skin. Eager to lick her sensitive spots and hear her moan his name in pleasure. Yeah, that never got old.

She arched her back off the bed, rising to meet his descending lips. He kissed her with increasing ardor as he unhooked the bra behind her back and then slipped the straps off her shoulders. She shrugged and the rest of it fell away. He was too caught up in the kiss to notice when she flung her bra away so hard it flew across the room.

CHAPTER 14

This was what Evie had wanted. Skin on skin. Her mate's rough body against hers, with nothing between them. Oh, they'd made love since he'd been back, but facing such danger today, side by side, had added some heretofore unknown element to their lovemaking. It wasn't desperation—not in the bad sense, anyway. It was more like a knowing that their time together was finite. It was an urgency that pushed her to jump his bones the way she'd been contemplating pretty much ever since the battle had ended.

And now…she had him where she'd dreamed of having him. In their bed. Naked. And he was doing his best to drive her absolutely stark raving wild.

Evie couldn't take much more of Ray's touch. His teasing. His absolute knowledge of what would make her most likely to lose all inhibitions and sense of propriety. She was very close now. Just a few more of those licking, nibbling kisses on the tender skin of her breasts, and she was going to lose it.

Then, he bit her—gently, but it was definitely a bite—and she totally lost it. She growled, letting her wolf show as she tugged at Ray's strong shoulders until he rolled, letting her push him down onto the bed. She straddled him, unable to hold off any longer. With little fanfare, she took his long, hard cock into her body, seating herself on him with a sense of relief. Oh, yeah. That's what she'd wanted. She didn't feel quite so empty now, though she was still straining toward the height of pleasure only Ray could give her.

Gaining confidence as she began to roll her hips, feeling him in her most intimate places, she closed her eyes for a long moment, just enjoying the sensations. When Ray's hands went to her hips, guiding her movements, she opened her eyes, gazing down at him and melting a little inside at the indulgent look of utter love on his face.

As much as she might look the aggressor here, she knew that he was allowing her this time on top. He was giving her wolf—and her woman side—what they needed. Him. In whatever way she wanted him.

She'd thought she couldn't love him any more than she already did, but then, he went and did something like this, and she found there was still another tiny, little, previously unknown part of her heart he hadn't managed to claim yet. Who was she kidding? Her heart was his. Totally and completely. And had been for a very long time.

There was no sense in thinking anything else. Ray might've been missing in action for the past twenty years, but never once, in all that time, had she given up on him. Or given up loving him with everything that was in her.

He was hers. It was just that simple. And she was his.

That was the last coherent thought she had for some time as she bounced up and down on his dick, feeding the need of her body for the pleasure that could only be gained from his. She was feeding the need in her soul at the same time—the need for the closeness sharing their bodies with each other created.

Their magic sparked and swirled around the cabin as usual, but she supposed she was getting used to it at this point, and it didn't distract her. In fact, the pulsing light show helped regulate her movements. As the sparkling intensity increased, so did her movements until, finally, she blew apart, even as the light culminated in an explosion of fireworks visible only to them, within the safe confines of their little love nest.

Ray climaxed with her, she knew. Both from the physical evidence of his body tensing under hers and from the way their magic exploded together in a magical storm of symmetry.

Exhausted on the physical, mental, and magical planes, Evie lowered herself to lay over her lover—a warm, living blanket. She thought about moving off him, but his arms anchored her in place, and she didn't have the energy to argue. She felt Ray tug a blanket over them both a few minutes later, and then, warmed by her mate under her and a soft blanket over her, she slept the sleep of the well-pleasured and weary.

Hours later, Ray woke before both Evie and the sun. It was the still dark hour before dawn when he opened his eyes and took stock of his situation. Evie was warm and naked in his arms. He loved that. Loved being with her after all that time apart.

The wards—what was left of them—were quiet. He sent his magical senses out, a tendril of his consciousness testing the air currents around the cabin in all directions. All was secure. It had snowed a little more overnight, though nothing like the blizzard of their first day here. In the fresh snow, only the prints of small animals and those creatures that were native to this land shone. All was well.

On an internal level, Ray's magic was restored. It wasn't one hundred percent yet. That would take a while, still. But it was much, much better. They could go back and face the music in Pennsylvania today. He was definitely strong enough to port them both there quickly and as quietly as possible.

The question was—did he really want to leave their honeymoon cabin on the edge of the res? Out here, he could almost make himself believe that not much time had passed since they'd last been together. He could almost forget the years of torture and imprisonment in the fey realm. He could almost—just almost—forget that he had a grown son he'd never really met.

That burned when he thought about it. He'd missed so much. His son's entire life to this point. Although it sounded like Josh had turned out to be a man any father would be proud of, Ray was devastated by the thought that he hadn't been there for him, or for Evie. He'd let his mate down in the worst possible way.

The only thing that would have been worse, was if he'd left them of his own volition. If he'd run out on them, he would have counted himself the worst sort of slime. As it was, he questioned his actions back then that had led to his imprisonment. Had he been too much of a glory hound, thinking himself invincible and taking risks that he should never have taken? Had he been responsible—in the final analysis—for his own entrapment and the horrid circumstances that had left his mate and his unborn son all alone out in the wild?

He hated to think that might just be the case.

He would have to work for the rest of his long life to earn Evie's and Josh's forgiveness. That Evie had already forgiven him didn't matter. He would still work to be worthy of her love for the rest of his days. He could do no less.

Walking away from her—even if he believed it would be the best thing to do—wasn't an option. Ray was just selfish enough to want to continue to be with her, no matter that he didn't really deserve her. Or the overwhelming joy and happiness she brought to his life.

Evie stretched in his arms and made those soft little sounds that were a prelude to her waking. He loved watching her wake up, opening her eyes and then smiling at him. How he'd missed that all those years apart. The simple acts of being together. The day-to-day intimacies.

"Mmm. Good morning," she murmured, stretching even more in his arms. Her eyes were little slits as she woke up gradually.

"It snowed a little more overnight," he told her gently.

She made no comment, still waking up, that kittenish look doing things to his heart. She was really the most incredibly beautiful woman, in all her guises.

"I was thinking…" He paused, unsure, now that the moment was upon him, about ending their time together all alone out here in North Dakota. He wasn't sure he wanted to go back and share Evie with anyone just yet. Even their grown son and his new mate.

"Yeah?" Evie prompted. "Come on, Ray. You know you can tell me anything."

He sighed and shook his head. "Well, I was thinking that we should probably go back and see Josh and Deena now that my magic is mostly restored. Before the magical eddies settle too much. Just in case anyone is still out there watching this area."

She looked at him with a rapidly changing expression. She went from joy to sadness, then resolution and pride. He thought he understood. She wanted to see Josh, but then, she probably thought—like Ray had—about ending their alone time. But it had to be done. They had to face their son at some point, and sooner would probably be better than later.

She probably had also figured out how much Ray feared what Josh might have to say to him after all these years, despite Duncan's assertions that Josh understood. There was no way around the fact that Ray had been absent through his son's entire life up to this point. There was no easy way to jump into the role of father now. And Ray suspected there would be at least some resentment on Josh's part. Who could blame him? It must've been hard growing up without a dad.

Ray had so much regret. The fact that Ray's absence hadn't been deliberate didn't really count for much to Ray's way of thinking. His choices had led to his imprisonment. His choice to serve the Lady and to fight Her enemies had led to the trap that had kept him from his mate and son. There was no way around it. If Ray were in Josh's place, he'd be harboring a whole lot of anger against his absentee dad.

Maybe that's why Evie was looking at him with pride in her pretty brown eyes. Maybe she was proud that he was willing to face the music, instead of hiding out here at the cabin even longer.

"As long as you think you can get us there in one piece, I think it's a good idea," she told him, smiling gently, though eagerness to be on their way shone in her sparkling eyes. He remembered how much the wolf inside her liked going places.

"All right." He took a deep breath, already thinking of what they'd have to do to prepare for their journey. "We can go after we tidy up the cabin and put things back to rights."

Plan firmly in mind, they ate breakfast then began cleaning the cabin in earnest. Evie instructed him in the proper way to prep the place to sit empty for a while. It was just possible that they wouldn't get back here this season, so everything had to be shut down and winterized—as they had found it when they ported in.

Ray turned off the generator and followed Evie's instructions on how to leave everything in the little shed that housed the machine. He found the stock of antifreeze and did as she told him with that, as well, in the plumbing. They worked together to make certain no food was left out where rodents could get at it, and that all containers were shut tight and put away behind closed cabinet doors.

When everything was secure, Ray and Evie went outside to lock the door and board things up against any of the more persistent wildlife that might wander out this way. Once that was done and everything was as prepared as they could make it, Ray took Evie by the hand and led her a short distance from the cabin.

She had phoned Josh earlier to tell him of their plans, and Ray had talked briefly with Deena about his intention to use the stone circle on her land as the terminus for his port. She had agreed that it was the safest place to avoid detection by anyone who might be watching for energy ripples.

Then, as the afternoon sun shone down on them and they faced the cabin that had been their honeymoon home, Ray took Evie in his arms and called on his magic. A moment later, the cabin faded, and an altar of living rock stood before them, surrounded by standing stones that embraced his energies and redirected any leftover eddies of magical current down into the earth. Perfect.

With any luck, nobody would be able to detect their arrival through magical means.

Ray released Evie from his tight hold and let her go. She immediately went over to the perimeter of the circle to greet the tall man and much shorter woman who waited just outside. Josh and Deena.

Ray would make his hellos soon, but just for a moment, he needed a chance to regroup. He hadn't been in the mortal world in a while, and the flow of magic was different here than in faerie. Plus, his magic was enough to get them here, but the expenditure of power at this stage in his healing from all those years of being drained left him a little light-headed.

All that, plus the fact that he was just grateful to be alive and with his mate once more—and now, his son… The moment was a bit harrowing emotionally.

Ray sank to one knee before the altar stone and lifted up a prayer of thanks to the Mother of All. He had a lot to be grateful for.

He shut his eyes, taking the moment he needed to gather his strength—magical, physical and emotional. Taking a deep breath, he opened his eyes and stood. It was time to face his son.

Ray turned and walked toward the small group at the edge of the circle of standing stones. Evie was there, tears in her eyes as she smiled, looking between Ray and their son, an eager sort of anticipation on her expressive face. The other woman looked happy, too, though Ray could see the wetness shining in her eyes even as she smiled. This must be Deena, the priestess his son had mated.

And the man… The child was forever lost to Ray, but the man looking back at him had his mother's eyes. The same wild wolf that lived in Evie's pure soul also inhabited Josh's. But he was as tall as Ray was, and his muscular shape looked very much like what Ray saw in a mirror when he cared to look. Tall, broad of shoulder, arms that could heft a sword, a lithe build that meant he could move well when called upon to fight.

Yes, this was familiar to Ray. Josh could very well be a chip off the old block, but Ray knew whatever his son had achieved, it had been through no help from Ray. He'd been absent his son's whole life, which wasn't fair to either of them.

Ray walked up to Josh, facing him, like mirror images, only one was half-werewolf and one was fully fey. They had a lot in common, but it was their differences that would be the most interesting to Ray—if Josh gave his sire a chance to get to know him.

"Joshua," Ray said simply, trying very hard not to let his voice crack with emotion.

"Father," Josh acknowledged, in a harsh tone that made Ray want to flinch.

"You have every right to hate me. I wasn't there for you or your mother, but we cannot change the past, no matter how much I wish it possible. Can you ever forgive me?"

Josh stepped a little closer, his posture less severe. "There is nothing to forgive," he said in a strained tone.

Ray had chosen not to speak to Josh by phone while he and Evie had been in North Dakota. He'd left the communicating to Evie, preferring to speak to his son for the first time face to face. Josh had felt the same, Evie had told him.

Ray was glad they'd waited now. Context was everything, and body language spoke volumes. What he read from Josh's face, words and stance was better than anything he could have hoped for. It was just possible that his son didn't hate him, after all, though Ray really wouldn't have blamed him if he had.

"Thank you both for freeing me," Ray said, including Deena in his words.

Deena stepped forward, aligning herself with her mate. "I'm so glad to finally meet you," Deena said, moving forward to hug Ray.

He returned the hug, grateful his son had found a woman with such a big heart. If she was willing to accept him so easily, perhaps his son would come to find a similar ease with him in time.

When Deena stepped back, she put her arm around Josh's waist, urging him forward. "My mate has been looking forward to talking to you about his new calling."

"It fills my heart with joy and pride to know that the Mother of All has chosen you to serve, Josh," Ray admitted.

It seemed the right thing to say. Josh moved a step closer.

"I was angry with you for a long time," Josh admitted. "But I understand now. You couldn't do anything other than what you did. You were serving your calling. You didn't leave us on purpose. And Deena seems to think…" His voice had dropped lower with each word, and he hesitated, looking at his mate, as if for reassurance. She nodded, urging him on as strong emotion rolled off Josh in waves so palpable, even Ray could feel them. "Deena thinks everything happened this way by the Goddess's design. Though I can't imagine why putting Mom through so much pain and uncertainty was something the Lady wanted."

"Josh!" Evie chastised him, but not angrily. She was sniffling now, but not sad. More just overcome by the moment. "The past is behind us. The future is always uncertain. We need to just enjoy the moments we have now—finally being together as a family. The rest is all superfluous."

Ray put his right arm around Evie's waist, pulling her to his side and placing a kiss on top of her head. She had grown incredibly wise in the years they'd been kept apart.

"You're so right," Deena agreed with Evie's words.

Evie reached out with her free hand to their son, and Josh came to her. Deena then reached out to Ray, and he took her hand, completing the circle. It was the women who would bind them all together, who would break the barriers that men sometimes found hard to overcome. Evie drew Josh in as Deena did the same, and they were suddenly in a sort of huddle, linked together by each having an arm around two others' waists. A family of four powerful beings, communing silently as a unit, though the bonds of blood and love were strong.

Then, Deena and Evie drew away, leaving just Josh and Ray, facing each other, closer than they'd ever been. Ray opened his arms, hoping his son would embrace him, but unwilling to push Josh any further than he was prepared to go right now. Too many years apart had damaged the relationship they should have had. Ray would take whatever Josh was willing to give him. That he'd even come this far was a huge thing to Ray.

But Josh didn't hesitate. He embraced his father for the first time, bringing tears to Ray's eyes and a momentary clash of magic as their energies—both powerful and strong—got used to each other. The flavor of Josh's magic was familiar but completely unique in the combination of werewolf and fey that comprised his son's true nature.

Ray laughed between the tears. This was his son. His son!

CHAPTER 15

Long moments later, after Ray had gotten a handle on his emotions somewhat, they broke apart. Josh's eyes were wet, too, and his smile was just as shaky as Ray's. It looked like his son was just as uncomfortable with *the mushy stuff*, as Evie would call it, as Ray was.

"Your magic is really wild and free, isn't it?" Ray observed, shaking his head as his grin became steadier.

"It was even worse before," Josh admitted, also seeming to regain some of his composure as time rolled on. "Deena has been a huge help there."

"Your mother tells me the fey magic just came upon you suddenly a few months back. I'm sorrier than I can say that you had to deal with that all on your own. It must've been quite the surprise."

"Yeah, you could say that." Josh shot a teasing look at his mother. "Especially considering Mom never mentioned that my father was fey."

"She what?" Ray looked at Evie, truly surprised.

"I, uh…" Evie began, looking a bit sheepish—which was hard for a werewolf. "I found it really difficult to talk about you, Ray."

Ray's heart contracted a bit, realizing the depth of the pain his absence must have caused her. Had she been so deep in grief that she couldn't even tell their son about his father?

When he considered the fact that many shifters didn't survive the loss of a mate, he guessed he shouldn't have been surprised. In fact, Evie had done remarkably well to raise their son all on her own and continue to live her life—even when she thought her mate was gone from this world.

He knew that many shifters chose to follow their mates into death, regardless of the circumstances or who they left behind. If Evie had chosen that route, not only might Josh never have been born, but Ray wouldn't have been on the other side of the veil, waiting for her. He'd been trapped in faerie, not dead.

Something deep inside Evie had known that he wasn't really dead all along. Some instinct had kept her alive and allowed their son to be born and grow into a formidable man.

Ray drew Evie close once again and hugged her to his side. "It's okay, Evie. I understand." He would forgive her anything. Absolutely anything. All that mattered was that they were together again now. The past was over, as she'd said. Now was all that mattered.

"I didn't," Josh admitted. "Not really." He looked significantly at Deena. "Not until I found my own mate and realized what it must've cost you to even think about my father." He was talking directly to his mother now, with Ray and Deena as witnesses. "I get it, Mom. I do."

Tears were running down Evie's cheeks as she left Ray's side to hug their son. Josh was a head taller than his mother, his bulk making Evie look small and delicate by contrast. That their son was a behemoth like his father warmed Ray's heart, though he would've been happy no matter what Josh looked like. The fact that Ray had a child of any kind was still sort of mind-blowing.

Ray watched mother and son, thinking again about how much he'd missed. He glanced over at Deena and found her watching him with compassion in her sparkling eyes. She had a kind spirit that shone clear in her aura. A woman of immense power, she was also one with a generous heart. Josh had been blessed with such a mate, and Ray looked forward to getting to know his new daughter-in-law better as time marched on. If the Goddess allowed.

Though, after so many years away from his family, he prayed the Mother of All would see fit to let him be here for them now. He'd missed so much.

"Shall we go back to the house? It's warmer inside," Deena invited as Josh and Evie broke apart.

"It's balmy here compared to where we just left," Ray assured her, glad to leave the emotional stuff behind for a few minutes and think about more mundane things.

Evie walked with Josh as they headed back toward the farmhouse. She understood that it would take time for father and son to be comfortable around one another. It was both painful and joyful to watch them trying to figure out where they stood with each other so early in this new relationship. She'd always wanted Josh to know his father but had never really thought it possible.

This—seeing them together, finally—was a dream come true for Evie. She sent a little prayer skyward that their relationship would only improve and grow deeper the longer they knew each other.

Deena told Ray about the farm as they approached the big white house. Evie could feel the joy in the structure. Some houses just felt happy, and this one definitely had that vibe going on. Due, she was sure, to the happy couple who now lived there.

The fact that Josh had, in essence, moved to Pennsylvania permanently to be with his mate was something Evie was still trying to sort out in her own mind. She understood why it would be much harder for Deena to relocate than Josh. It only made sense that Josh be the one to change locations. Deena was, after all, a priestess given watch over a sacred site.

The standing stones they had just left might not be as tall or impressive as the monoliths in North Dakota, but they were every bit as powerful and needful of protection. Deena watched over these stones as Fred was the caretaker of the striped stone circle in his territory. Such caretakers didn't just up and move when the mood struck them.

Also, Deena had to be near the stones and within the safety of the borders and wards of her farm because of her link with the Goddess. She was a strong priestess with a special gift that needed to be protected, which is why she didn't get out much, and couldn't stray far from her home.

The fact that Sir Duncan had been coming to the farm to train Josh in the ways of Knighthood was telling. If such a powerful and important personage as a fey Knight of the Light was adjusting his schedule to be in rural Pennsylvania, then Deena's need to be here trumped the usual arrangement of the student traveling to meet the teacher and not vice versa.

The house welcomed them as it had the first time Evie had seen it. She imagined that the house that had been mostly empty until now was rejoicing in all the new people and relationships under its protective roof. If homes had a personality—which Evie believed they did—this one was definitely happy. And getting happier with each new person it sheltered under its roof.

There were still a few days until the Winter Solstice, which meant that Evie and Ray still had a day or two with Josh and Deena before Deena's relatives started arriving to celebrate the holiday with her. That was another telling thing. Deena's family traveled to her—and apparently did so all the time. Evie hadn't once heard Deena talk about going to visit her family. Only of them coming to see her.

"I can introduce you to the animals tomorrow, if you like," Deena told Ray. "They're as much part of my family as the rest of the tribe that's due to arrive in a couple of days. I hope you won't be overwhelmed by them." Deena laughed, and Evie noticed Ray looking slightly uncomfortable.

She'd always known him to be a social animal, but he'd been out of circulation for a long time. Evie supposed Ray would take a bit of time to get used to being around people again, but luckily, the members of Deena's family were well acquainted with magic and the need for secrecy.

They also knew about fey. After all, Deena's great-grandmother many times over was fey.

"Isn't your great-grandmother coming for the holiday?" Evie asked. She hadn't wanted to pry for particulars before, but now that Ray was back, it seemed less rude somehow to ask for more detail.

Deena shrugged as she invited them to sit by gesturing toward the couch in the large living room. "I'm never sure if she'll be able to make it or not, but she said she'd try. She wants to meet Josh."

Deena's smile for Josh was full of love, and Evie was happy to see it. She knew her son was fully committed to the young priestess, and it was good to know that, even if Deena wasn't were and therefore might not feel the same deep bond that Evie and Josh felt when their wolves saw their mates, Deena was nonetheless deeply in love with Josh. It shone in her eyes and her words every time she spoke of Josh, which warmed Evie's heart.

Evie sat on the couch, Ray beside her. She took his hand and placed their entwined fingers on his knee. "I only ask because I was wondering if Ray would have some fey company or if he'd be the odd man out."

"Oh! Don't worry about that. My family is all half-fey, and some manifest the fey magic more than others. There are a few married-in shifters and human mages, of course, but all my blood relations carry fey magic. You won't stand out too much, Sir Rayburne."

"Just Ray, please, or Dad, if you prefer." Ray gave a quirky smile as he seemed to try out the term. "I'll have to get used to that, but I really do like the sound of it," he mused.

"I suspect Duncan will be along tomorrow or the next day," Josh put in after a moment's silence had passed, charged with emotion on Ray's part. "He had something to do in New York but promised he'd be back as soon as he could," Josh told Ray.

"That's good," Ray said. "I'd enjoy a chance to talk more with him. Everything has changed so much since I was last here. It's good to have a few touchstones to remind me that I'm not a stranger in a strange land." Ray squeezed Evie's hand and smiled at her.

"Everything else may change," she whispered to him, leaning in to kiss his cheek, "but my love remains constant."

He returned her kiss with one of his own. "Same here," he told her before withdrawing. "But let's not embarrass the younger generation." He chuckled, and they all laughed.

They ate together as a family that night. Deena had prepared a delicious meal, which Josh helped with by firing up what looked like a new grill on the back porch. Werewolves were carnivores, and Evie was glad of the rare steaks her son grilled for them, though Deena didn't partake, and Ray only ate a human-sized portion.

Evie and Ray shared the guest room that night, and she was happy to have access to her suitcases once again. Finally, she could get to her new clothes—not the discards she'd relegated to the cabin. They'd have to do some shopping for Ray, but for now, he was getting by with Josh's old stuff that had been at the cabin.

The next morning, Evie slept in. Ray was long gone by the time she woke up, and after a quick shower and change into one of the nice outfits she'd brought for her trip, she went to look for him. She found him in the farmyard with Josh, doing some kind of martial art with sticks in their hands.

No. Not sticks. Swords. Sticks that represented swords, at least. They weren't practicing with live steel or the magical glowing swords Evie had seen Ray wield during the battle, but she recognized some of the moves. Ray was teaching Josh a sword form in slow motion.

Evie just stood quietly and watched the moment of bonding between father and son.

Until a car drove up the gravel driveway.

As the dust cloud blew away, a man emerged from the

sleek silver car. It was Duncan, Knight of the Light and brother in arms to Ray, and now Josh. Evie held her breath, wondering what would happen next.

CHAPTER 16

Ray recognized the feel of Duncan's power before he even saw his face. Duncan had returned, as promised.

Ray put down the sticks, which had stood in for the swords he favored, and strode forward to meet Duncan, who was emerging from the slickest car Ray had ever seen. It looked like a spaceship, but then again, styles had been quite different the last time Ray had been in the mortal realm. He had a lot of catching up to do as far as human technology went. But that was for later.

Duncan spoke first. "Good to see you again, my friend. How goes it here?"

"Well enough," Ray replied. He'd thought of quite a few questions he wanted to ask Duncan since their last brief meeting in North Dakota. "I've been wondering. The last I heard, long ago, nobody knew where you were, and the worst was feared. What happened to you back then? You just disappeared. Long before I made my own abrupt exit." Ray placed one hand on Duncan's back.

"I was trapped in faerie, much like you," Duncan explained.

Ray frowned. "We'll have to compare notes so nothing of the kind ever happens to either of us—or anyone else we know—again."

They walked slowly away from the car and back toward the barnyard where Ray had been checking what his son knew about sword work. Little, as it turned out, but Josh showed every sign of being a good student, and he wasn't too old to learn. If he applied himself, he'd be a credible swordsman in time. Ray would make sure of it.

Duncan chuckled as he caught sight of the matching sticks still in Josh's hands. "Teaching him your impossible two-sword form?"

Ray gave his friend a mock-insulted look. "It's not impossible for me."

"Of course not, you're a freak!"

Ray's laugh boomed out, surprising himself, as well as the onlookers. It felt so good to be with a friend and equal again. Someone who could call him on his bullshit and laugh with him at their shared past. The dual swords he affected had often been a bone of contention between them, in a friendly way.

It took dedication to master the off-hand so that there was no weakness in the two-sword approach. Ray had spent decades perfecting his form and working to make himself as ambidextrous as possible. No other Knight he knew of used the dual swords, but Ray was just conceited enough to consider it his signature style, and he hoped—pride made him hope—that his son might take after him and follow the same path, in time.

"I've been teaching Josh single-sword styles, like any *normal* person," Duncan went on in the face of Ray's laughter.

Ray relented. "As well you should," he agreed magnanimously. "The sword set is something it will take him years to master, but I just wanted to see if he might have the aptitude."

"And does he?" They came to a stop, facing Josh, who was watching them with a very interested gaze. The boy missed nothing, which made Ray proud all over again.

"He's strong enough on both sides. Close to ambidextrous now. I think it'll come to him even easier than it did to me,"

Ray admitted, beaming.

"Surely, you jest," Duncan protested, but he was smiling while he did so.

Josh stepped forward, offering his right hand for Duncan to shake in greeting. "As a wolf, I don't favor either set of paws," he said, winking as he grinned.

"Damn and blast. Are you telling me your wolf side is already ambidextrous?" Duncan asked, pretending to huff.

"That's about the size of it. I've used my right as a human mostly so I could just fit in with the rest of the world."

"That's cheating. Isn't it?" Duncan asked, seeking support for his contention and finding none. Ray just shook his head, enjoying the friendly banter.

They talked of simple things for a while until Deena and Evie left them alone for a bit. Then, the serious talk began. Talk of warfare, weaponry, training and skill.

Stars, how he'd missed this. The camaraderie of his brother Knights was something Ray had always enjoyed. Not that there ever were many Knights at a given time. Unless they were fey, they didn't last. Ray had befriended, then mourned, more of his brethren than he cared to count over the centuries, but it was good to see Duncan again. And it was good to know that Ray's son would share in this special legacy.

For though Josh was half-shifter, he was also half-fey, with a power greater than Ray had honestly expected. It was very likely his son would have a greatly extended lifespan, barring death in battle or misadventure. Ray was glad of that. He'd buried too many of his brother Knights. The sorrow would be even greater—though it was always bad to lose someone—if Josh perished too soon in this dangerous calling.

Which was why Ray vowed to train Josh to be the very best he possibly could be. Ray would have to have a serious talk with Evie soon about logistics. It was pretty clear that Josh was going to be based here for the time being. Ray felt he would have to find a way to be here—in rural

Pennsylvania, of all places—as well.

Duncan, Ray and Josh spent the day together, discovering what Josh already knew and the areas he would need to work on. They broke for lunch when the ladies brought a feast of sandwiches and juice out to them, but otherwise, they worked the day through. Deena meandered around the yard a bit, working with her animals, but though the alpacas kept eyeing the trio of men exercising in the barnyard, none of Deena's creatures interfered.

Ray saw Evie sneaking around in wolf form at least twice. She'd probably wanted to check the boundaries of Deena's farm for herself, which was a sensible thing to do. She probably also wanted to spy on her mate and son a bit, which Ray didn't mind at all. He did his best to hide his little grin when he sensed her presence, preferring to let her think she could sneak around unseen—at least for the moment. He'd pounce on her later. When they got a moment alone.

The men washed up as the sun began to descend and made their way indoors. Duncan was given the use of another guest room that lay ready for the arrival of Deena's family. They weren't expected to start arriving until tomorrow, so the room was available for Duncan, which was just as well. The three men had put in a full day's work, and each needed a shower before showing up for dinner.

In Ray's case, he spent a few stolen moments in the warm downpour with his mate, reacquainting himself with shower sex. Truly one of the great conveniences of this realm. Warm water maintained without the use of magic and the slippery skin of his perfect mate. Life didn't get much better than that.

Understandably, Evie and Ray were the last to arrive in the dining room, but nobody said anything. A few looks passed among them until Evie blushed and Ray pulled her into his side, telling the rest of them to cut it out. Laughter ensued, and all was right with the world as Evie joined in, smiling through her embarrassment.

Duncan joined them for the meal, offering a few bottles of wine he'd brought with him in the slinky sports car he'd driven down from New York City. Ray took a sip and thought he sensed a familiar flavor.

"Don't tell me Maxwell is still making wine." Ray reached for the bottle in the center of the table, turning it around so he could see the label.

"His winery is one of the best," Duncan confirmed. "He's won all sorts of awards."

"No kidding." Ray shook his head, surprised. "He still in California?"

Duncan nodded. "Napa Valley. He and a few of his friends have turned it into a wine-making capital to rival some parts of Europe."

"The deuce you say," Ray scoffed, but took another sip. "He hasn't lost his touch. In fact, this is better than his earlier vintages."

"Took him a century to get the grapes just right," Duncan said, nodding.

"A century?" Deena asked, her eyes wide. "Is he fey?"

Duncan nearly choked but regained his composure easily. "Sorry. No. He's a bloodletter. Good guy, for all that he drinks only blood...and wine."

"Bloodletter?" Deena looked confused for a moment until the term seemed to click in her mind. "You mean, one of the world's top vintners is a vampire?"

"They don't like that word," Duncan told her gently, "but yes. Atticus Maxwell is a vampire and a force for good...and excellent wine. I've known him a long time. As has the friend I'm currently house-sitting for. Dante is another vampire, as you call them. But he's on his honeymoon with his werewolf mate."

Ray realized the implications of what Duncan was saying, even if the others didn't. That the races were beginning to inter-mix again could mean dire things for the world at large. For the past few centuries, since the defeat of Elspeth, the magical races had stayed mostly to themselves. Bloodletters didn't mix with shifters and never with fey. Drinking shifter blood made the average vampire incredibly powerful. Fey blood was even more dangerous, imparting massive amounts of magical energy to a being that was already very strong.

In the normal course of business, the Goddess didn't really allow for such pairings. After all, She was the one who guided those fated to be mates together. If there was no call for beings of such power, then those kinds of matings tended not to happen. At all.

That an ancient vampire—and Dante was someone Ray remembered from a very long time ago—had found his One, true mate, among the shifters was very significant. Ray supposed the cross-species mating had started with himself and Evie, but theirs wasn't as uncommon a combination. Fey could mate with humans, though it was often heartbreaking for the fey involved when their human lover died of old age. Fey often found companionship with longer-lived shifters, though matings such as Evie's and Ray's weren't quite as common.

Bloodletters most often found their One, after centuries of searching, among humans. Not since Elspeth had been wreaking her havoc on the mortal realm had a bloodletter truly mated with a shifter. Not to Ray's knowledge. And bloodletters mating with fey had been strictly forbidden, though during the battle with Elspeth, it had taken such a partnership to send the enemy to the farthest realms of existence. It had killed the bloodletter and her fey mate to do it, but they'd managed the incredible feat of magic...together.

"We're living in interesting times again, it seems," Duncan went on while Ray's mind spun. Duncan raised his glass, and it felt like, in that moment, only they two, of all the people gathered around that dinner table, really understood the threat that lay just beyond the safety of this blessed house and this moment out of time.

The Mother of All increased the number of her Knights only when She knew they would be needed. Had Ray been so proud of his son's achievement only to have to worry that Josh would be sent into battle before he was fully trained?

Ray vowed to have that talk about relocating with Evie

before another sunrise. He had to be there for his son now, as he hadn't been there before. Ray had a lot of time to make up for with Josh and much to teach him about how to survive the threats he might face as a Knight of the Light.

Duncan left after dinner, though he'd been invited to stay overnight. He'd graciously turned over Josh's training to Ray with words of encouragement and happiness. He'd also agreed to check back with them from time to time as Josh's training progressed. Duncan could be of great help, even if he wasn't to be Josh's primary teacher.

They stayed up late talking after Duncan left, but eventually, everybody said goodnight and headed for their rooms. Now was the time, Ray knew, that he had to talk with Evie about where they would live. He didn't think she'd object to moving closer to their son, but he was working hard at remembering he was part of a couple.

For so many years, whatever decisions he'd had to make while trapped in faerie—and there hadn't been many—he'd made on his own. He'd been alone there, but for his tormentor.

But now, he was back in the mortal realm and had Evie's feelings and plans to consider. He loved that. He loved being part of a couple, even though it meant a slight delay in finalizing and implementing plans because he had someone to talk things over with. How he'd missed that. How he'd missed her.

As they entered the guest suite they were sharing on one side of the big farmhouse, Ray took the opportunity to broach the subject. He wanted her full agreement and input. They were a team. They would make the important decisions like this, as a team.

"If I'm going to be teaching Josh," he began, pausing just inside the doorway, "it would be a whole lot easier if we were nearby."

Evie turned to look at him, a smile on her face. "I'm glad you brought that up. I was wondering when you'd get around to asking me what I thought."

"Oh, honey, don't be like that." He smiled, moving in on her, then wrapping his hands around her waist, pulling her closer. "I planned this all out. I wanted to talk to you in private first before I made any stupid assumptions and blurted them out in front of everyone. We should present a united front, shouldn't we?"

"Hmph." She gave him a sly look. "That was your master plan?" He could tell she was just teasing him. She wasn't really mad, which was a relief. They hadn't been back together long enough to fight over something they probably both agreed on, anyway.

"Well, it was a plan. Not sure if it was masterful." He shrugged as she chuckled.

"When Duncan started talking about how you were going to take over Josh's training, I kind of figured a move might be in order. Deena's tied to this land for the moment. She can't just up and move to wherever. Josh explained a bit of that to me already. It's why he moved in here, rather than them finding a place together somewhere else," Evie explained. "If Deena's tied to this location and Josh is bound to Deena, then it only makes sense that, in order to teach him, you'd have to do it here. And I suppose commuting from North Dakota is probably out of the question."

"Not entirely." Ray tilted his head, knowing he needed to give Evie all the facts. "I could port in and out if Fred and Deena don't object to my using the standing stones for cover. It's risky. Any one of my ports could cause a ripple that our enemies might trace back to us, but I could theoretically travel back and forth every few days. The big problem with that scenario is that either you would travel with me or I would have to leave you behind in North Dakota, on your own for days at a time. I really don't want to do that. We've been apart long enough. And that's all presupposing you want to live at the cabin in Fred's territory and he's agreeable to my use of the stone circle."

"I live much closer to town now, actually," Evie said,

almost offhandedly.

"I don't suppose there's a convenient set of standing stones near your new home?" He had to chuckle because such things were rare, indeed.

"Not that I'm aware of," Evie told him with a shake of her head. "But I agree. I don't want to be separated from you either, and I don't like the idea of commuting back and forth. The danger of discovery is a problem, but I also don't like the idea of never knowing where I'm going to be from one day to the next. My wolf likes to know the bounds of her territory. She needs a sense of belonging in one place."

"Then, have you given any thought to relocating somewhere nearby?" Ray asked, hopeful. "We could buy our own place around here somewhere and be on hand for Josh and Deena when they need us, but still have our own home. Our own territory. How does that sound?"

Evie hugged him. "I think it sounds just about perfect."

He kissed her, then, as he backed her toward the big bed. He lay her down upon it and showed her all over again how much he loved her.

They made love several times that night, sleeping sporadically, but it was enough. It was enough for Evie just to be in her mate's arms, safe in his embrace, having him here with her, where he belonged. Where they lived didn't matter as much as that they lived together, in the same realm of existence.

Just before dawn, she woke him with nibbling kisses all over his chest...and lower. She took him into her mouth, rousing him in every way. She loved how responsive he was to her, even after he'd claimed she'd tired him out completely.

Shifters were demanding lovers, which was part of the reason they didn't often mate outside their own species. Few humans could keep up. But Ray was proving the fey had every inch the sexual energy of any shifter...and more than most.

Ray flipped them over, his greater strength appealing to

her inner wolf. She liked that her mate was the Alpha in their relationship, though she knew theirs was a partnership, not a dictatorship. They were perfect together and had been since the day she'd first stumbled across him—a stranger in the small town near which she'd grown up.

Back in those days, she hadn't really liked being around humans all that much, but she'd had a part-time job in a convenience store, working the night shift. One dark night, Ray had walked in and changed her life forever. He'd recognized what she was right away, though she hadn't ever considered she'd meet a real live fey in her lifetime.

It had taken Ray a few days before he admitted what he was, and even longer before he told her about being a *Chevalier.* They'd already run away together, heading south, out of Canada, before he'd come clean about his commitment to the Mother of All. It had been okay, though. Evie had always had a strong respect for the Goddess and counted herself blessed to have a mate who not only respected Evie's beliefs, but served the Goddess as a warrior for good. She'd been proud of her clever, skilled mate once she'd known.

But then, he'd disappeared, leaving her in a new country, pregnant and alone. She'd always known in her heart that he hadn't meant for anything like that to happen, but even so…

Ray distracted her from her twirling thoughts by the simple act of joining with her yearning body. He came into her, coming home. Making them whole.

Then, he began to move, and the sparks of magic began to swirl around them anew. They'd managed to tone down the light show over the past hours, but they still needed a bit of practice at keeping it completely under wraps.

Ray had cast a ward of protection around the room before he'd taken her to bed, making sure that any magic they did spark would be contained within the room. He'd explained that Deena had wards on the property itself and her home, but Ray was only being polite in containing their own magic within Deena's walls. Apparently, there were special rules for magical house guests that Evie had known nothing about.

Ray drove her to the stars, biting her shoulder at the end, making her inner wolf want to howl in joy. He might've picked that little biting thing up from her, but as long as he didn't mind, she certainly wasn't going to complain. Far from it. She loved it when he got all primal on her. Ray might be fey, but he was definitely a warrior when it counted, and that appealed to her on every level.

CHAPTER 17

Deena's family started showing up the next morning. They showed up in a big ol' rented minivan, driven by a young man who looked human but had the distinct whiff of magic about him. When he jumped out of the minivan and immediately grabbed Deena for an off-the-ground whirling hug, Josh stopped what he was doing to watch with narrowed eyes and a small growl that only Ray could hear.

They'd been out in the barnyard practicing sword forms since the sun had risen, getting in a few hours of work before the relatives showed up, but Ray hadn't counted on them arriving so soon. Ray took Josh's practice swords—sticks that Ray had whittled down to the approximate size and shape of swords to use until they had suitable equipment sourced and sent here through circuitous channels—and prodded his son to go meet the in-laws.

"That better be her brother or he's going to lose a limb," Josh growled under his breath as Ray patted him on the back and sent him on his way.

Evie came over to watch the proceedings. She'd exited the house with Deena when they'd heard the minivan pull up, but like Ray, Evie had hung back to allow time for Deena to greet her family before springing the new in-laws on everybody. Ray put his arm around Evie's waist after he stowed the improvised practice swords into a corner of the barn where nobody would stumble across them accidentally.

They weren't dangerous or anything, but they did look more like swords than sticks now. Best to keep them away from those who might ask too many questions. Ray wasn't sure how open Deena or Josh could be about their callings with her family. In fact, he didn't know much about her family at all except that they were magical. Some were human, some were mages, and more than a few were servants of the Goddess.

"They look like a fun bunch," Evie observed, smiling as they watched Deena introduce Josh to her family.

"Good thing that tall one is Deena's little brother. Josh is rather protective," Ray observed wryly.

"The mating is new. The wolf is very protective. Especially now," Evie explained. "Cut him some slack."

"Oh, I wasn't criticizing. I know just how Josh feels. When I first saw you interacting with Fred, I wanted to rip him apart," Ray admitted.

Evie turned to look up at him, wonder on her pretty face. "Really?" She paused a beat, searching his expression. "I'm flattered." She turned back to watch the family reunion, but not before Ray caught a rather smug smile of satisfaction curve her lips.

It wasn't too much longer before Deena looked around and motioned Ray and Evie over to meet her family. Josh was off to one side, deep in conversation with the brother, so Ray and Evie got to meet the others first.

"This is my mother, Melanie, and my dad, Peter," Deena introduced them as they smiled and offered handshakes and hugs. "My sisters, Barbara and Laurie, and my aunt, Gladys, and her husband, Geoff."

Ray offered to help the men with the suitcases as Evie settled in for some girl talk with the ladies in the group. If Ray didn't miss his guess, each and every one of those females was a priestess at one level or another. All had that fey influence on their energies, as did the brother, who came over to help with the bags. Josh introduced him as Gabe, and Ray was able to take the younger man's measure a bit, through their handshake.

The other two men were married into the family line. They were both humans with magic of their own, though Ray would have to be around them a bit more before he could gauge how much power each of them could command. He could do it with a quick magical query, but that was considered rude among friends, and if these men were married into a family so heavily laden with priestesses, Ray was pretty sure they were all right. The Mother of All kept a special eye on Her servants, as he well knew. Ray had no doubt the Goddess had Her hand in both of the older ladies' marriages.

It didn't take long to bring in the bags and set them in the rooms Deena had prepared on the other side of the big farm house. Every spare inch was serving as guest space now that there were three other couples and three singles staying here with Josh and Deena, and a few more were expected to trickle in over the next day or two until everyone was gathered for the Solstice celebration.

The day was spent catching up with, and learning more about, Deena's family. Wedding plans were discussed in some detail, and when that kind of talk started, the men found excuses to go outside and do manly things.

"The last thing I want to do is talk about matching the tablecloths to the napkins," Geoff muttered as the five males went out into the cold of the day, ostensibly to check the barn and see if anything needed fixing.

Josh was greeted by the critters around the barn as if he was their papa, and he spent a few minutes patting noses and stroking coats. Ray stood back and watched, marveling at how the small herd of mismatched animals had come to welcome the protection of an apex predator.

"I've never seen anyone but my sister be so accepted by her little tribe. Even the other girls don't get that kind of reception," Gabe observed, leaning one foot on the fence rail a couple of feet from where Ray had stopped.

"Josh is their protector," Ray said. "And perhaps they sense the wild spirit in his own soul."

"But he's a wolf, right?" Gabe objected. "I've never seen anything like *that* before, between a predator and its prey." He gestured toward where the two alpacas were eagerly receiving scratches behind their fluffy little ears.

Ray had to chuckle as the female alpaca leaned forward to nibble on the ends of Josh's hair. She certainly was friendly toward a being she probably should've been running from. But then, the animals had probably learned over the past weeks that Josh was there to keep them from all harm, not cause it. What he hadn't really expected was that Josh would take to the animals as much as they apparently took to him. That had been surprising to Ray.

"My son is still very much a mystery to me, but even the simplest creatures can recognize friend from foe. He's won them over. How? I'm not really sure," Ray told him.

The other two men had finished wandering around the barnyard, gazing up at the roof and checking the hinges on everything, then circled back to the fence where Ray and Gabe leaned. They also leaned against the sturdy wooden split rail fence, their breath hanging in the air as a frosty cloud each time anyone spoke. The weather had turned overnight, and it was starting to feel downright chilly, but nobody seemed to mind. It was a glorious day with not a cloud in the sky and temperatures cold enough to send an invigorating chill through a man's skin.

"We really have no excuse to stay out here," Deena's father, Peter, observed. "Josh seems to have repaired anything that might've needed fixing. Usually, that's our job—and our excuse to get out from underfoot when the ladies want to chat on their own."

"I'm pretty sure they figured that out long ago, Pete," Deena's uncle, Geoff, replied. "Don't worry about it. If they want us to come back in, they know where to find us."

"But it's cold out here," Pete replied, grinning.

"That's easily remedied," Ray said, waving a hand and bringing a small bit of warm air from the surrounding area to puff gently around their little group.

It was a negligible use of magic that wouldn't draw any attention, especially as they were well within Deena's protective wards here, and the small kindness might help Ray make friends with the in-laws.

Three sets of eyes turned to look at Ray wearing various expressions of astonishment. Hmm. Maybe he'd overdone it? Or miscalculated how readily these men might accept Ray's magical nature? Probably the latter.

"You really are fully fey, aren't you?" Gabe blurted out. Of the three men, he seemed the least fearful.

"I'm afraid so." Ray frowned a bit, regretting drawing such attention now that his little trick hadn't gone over the way he'd intended.

"It's cool," Gabe replied nonchalantly. "Grandma does stuff like that all the time. It's just a little spooky to mere mortals who don't have that kind of command over the natural world. Weather work is a specialty among human mages. My dad is a potions master," Gabe nodded toward his father, Peter. "And Uncle Geoff specializes in teaching the younger generation about spell work."

"I taught you, didn't I?" Geoff scoffed back jokingly at his nephew.

Gabe had to be in his mid-twenties, but as the youngest of the family, he was treated as if he were the baby. Ray suspected they'd be in for a surprise if a crisis came their way. Gabe radiated a vast power that impressed Ray, now that he was close enough to feel it.

"That you did, Uncle Geoff, but you know my heart isn't really in reciting long litanies or chanting my head off. I'm a little more...uh...direct than that," Gabe complained, but Ray could see it was all in fun. The men of Deena's family had a good relationship vibe among them, which boded well for Josh's eventual acceptance among them.

Ray shook his head and sighed dramatically. "I don't think

Josh would sit still long enough for me to teach him spell work," Ray commiserated with Geoff. "At this stage, he's more a man of action, like young Gabe here. So, I'm teaching him sword work instead." Ray figured he might as well bring that out into the open since they'd probably seen Ray and Josh earlier that morning when the family had pulled in.

"I'd wondered about that," Peter admitted. "What's that all about? Is there a need for a werewolf mage to use a sword in this day and age?"

Josh must've heard because he came over, leaving the animals, though some of them followed at his heels, rubbing against his legs. They really loved him, and it was both heart-warming and amusing to watch.

"Deena and I talked about this…" Josh began. "And she decided it's not her place to say whether or not you're all told the exact nature of my power. You can confirm this with her, of course," Josh said politely, "but her intention is to let the Mother of All make that decision."

"What?" Peter looked confused.

"How?" Geoff asked at the same time.

"At our wedding. If the Goddess wills it, you'll all see my true nature. And if not, then we'll know for certain that some secrets are still to be kept," Josh finished mysteriously.

"Very cagey, young man," Peter said, giving Josh a side-eyed look.

"It's only fair though, Dad." Gabe came to Josh's defense, somewhat surprisingly. "The Mother of All will decide. That's the best way to go. You already know She wouldn't have allowed Deena to mate just anyone. Josh has already got the Goddess's blessing. That should be enough for us. Anything else is just curiosity on our parts and maybe not any of our business."

Ray felt his eyebrows rise as the young man spoke. Very wise words for one so young, he thought. This Gabe would bear watching. He had the fey blood, like the rest of his female kin. Perhaps he had a bit of empathy—or some higher calling—that would reveal itself in time.

Josh grinned. "Glad to hear you say that, Gabe. For now, I guess we'll just say my father is kind of an old guy, and back in his day, things were done with swords. Seeing as how we've only just met, I'm humoring the guy and learning something that's always intrigued me."

All eyes turned to study Ray again, and he did his best not to fidget. It was Gabe who broke the momentary silence.

"You're a full-blooded fey, which means you're pretty much immortal by human reckoning." Gabe's voice was hushed with wonder. "The things you must've seen. Were you really around during medieval times?"

Ray decided to indulge Gabe's curiosity. For one thing, he was trying to make friends of these people. For another, it was a good way to take the focus off what Josh might or might not be.

"Back in those days, it was much easier to travel between faerie and the mortal realm," Ray admitted. "I made regular visits here going back even further than that, but the most time I spent here was during the great war with the Destroyer. Humans call that time the Dark Ages. The only weapons we had back then were the old-fashioned kind. I fought with a dual sword style that few ever emulated, but Josh is doing well learning it. And I fought with magic, of course. Back then, mages were more plentiful, and the magic of this realm bubbled much closer to the surface."

Peter cleared his throat, drawing attention. "This seems like a natural point at which to confess that I looked you up in the family archive." His expression was a bit sheepish.

"Archive?" Josh asked. "Deena didn't mention her family had an archive."

Peter stood a bit straighter, no longer leaning against the fence. "My side of the family has been producing magical offspring since ancient times," he said with only a hint of pride in his voice. "The Llewellyn Archive is open to her, and to all my children, but she's never shown an interest in it."

"Wait a minute. Deena's family name is Llewellyn?" Ray asked as, suddenly, pieces of a puzzle he hadn't known he'd been working on clicked into place. He felt a grin coming on.

"Well, yeah," Josh said. "I thought you knew that."

"Actually, I didn't, but it explains a lot." Yes, he could feel the grin spreading over his face, but did nothing to stop it as he turned to Deena's father. "I knew a Peter Llewellyn many centuries ago. If I look closely, I see his influence. You have his shade of gray-blue eyes."

"Then, you really did know my ancestor?" The modern Peter seemed truly touched, his voice subdued.

"I knew him, respected him, and fought at his side many times over. He was a great man and a superior mage." Ray walked over to Peter and put one hand on his shoulder. "He was also a good friend."

A moment passed while Ray's words hung in the air between them. Peter placed his hand over Ray's.

"I hope we can also be friends. Especially considering that we're likely going to be sharing grandchildren." They all laughed then, and Ray let go of Peter's shoulder, moving back a bit.

Things were easier between them now. He could feel the bonds of friendship starting to form. It would still take time, but this was a very good start.

"So, what did it say about me in your archive?" Ray wanted to know.

"Well, there was a great deal of information written by my ancestor Peter about his friend, *Lord* Rayburne. He speculated that you were not of this realm, but he didn't seem to know for certain."

"Och, in those days, it was never wise to advertise if you were fey. The townsfolk didn't like my kind. It was a lot easier to cross the barrier between the realms back then, and some fey who came through did some rather nasty things here. Stealing children. Beguiling people's wives or husbands. Playing dirty tricks on the humans. A lot of the uncomplimentary old legends about fey have some basis in truth, unfortunately." Ray frowned.

"Are you really a lord?" Josh asked.

"In a manner of speaking. I was a fighting man, and back then, if you were good at that sort of thing and pledged your sword to a decent king, if you lived long enough, he'd give you a title and some land. I didn't live on the lands I was awarded for long, but I tried to be good to the people who lived there." Ray shrugged. "I didn't care much for titles, but it opened doors and helped me get things done back then. For one thing, it made it easier for me to raise a decent army when Elspeth's forces came against us. That's when I first met your ancestor, Peter. He was a powerful mage, and he came in with a fighting force of his own. All the members of his family were blessed with magic...and lots of it."

"So, not all of Deena's power comes from her fey great-grandmother," Josh observed, looking at Peter with new respect.

"No, not all," Peter said modestly. "Though you should know, I'll be adding your name to the family archive in due course," he warned Josh with a grin.

"Now, that's true immortality," Ray observed wryly and they all chuckled.

CHAPTER 18

Evie kept an eye on Ray out the window of the farmhouse when she could. The men seemed to be chatting near the barn, though it was cold enough outside that their breath made little clouds in front of their faces. Male bonding, she supposed.

The women had gotten down to serious wedding planning, including creating a kitchen schedule that boggled Evie's mind. They had everything planned down to the minute as to who would cook what and when. A shopping trip was being organized to pick up a two-page list of supplies they'd compiled, and Deena's mother and aunt had already volunteered their husbands to go along with them on the expedition to the local grocery store.

Evie was glad they weren't depending on her to contribute too much. She was feeling a little overwhelmed by the organized chaos of their conversation, and she realized she'd missed this after leaving home. Her Pack had been big and boisterous like this too. They'd had their good aspects, though her family's refusal to accept Ray had been the breaking point.

As a result, Evie had missed out on this sort of thing. She wouldn't have changed things. She'd gotten Josh, and he'd been more than enough for her. Now, she'd gotten Ray back, too, and her life was finally looking up once again. But watching Deena's family, she felt a little wistful too.

When the minivan left down the gravel drive carrying Deena and the rest of her family, along with the huge shopping list, Evie felt a little relieved. Ray had come back in with Josh, and they were eating a quick lunch of sandwiches before they went back out to take advantage of the relative quiet to get a bit more training in before the family came back with the supplies.

It was just the three of them—Josh, Ray and Evie—eating a quiet meal together while Deena went shopping with her family. Evie thought she'd have a bit of time to recover from the madness of the morning when Josh broached a subject she'd been dreading.

"Mom, do you have contact information for your parents?" Josh said, using his purposefully-nonchalant voice. She recognized it immediately, even as her stomach lurched at the question.

"Why?" she asked in reply, needing time to sort out her feelings before dealing with this emotionally charged topic.

"Deena was wondering if we shouldn't at least make them aware of our wedding. It seemed rude to her not to at least send an announcement. I told her you wouldn't go for it, but I did promise to at least ask." Josh was examining his sandwich as he explained, pretending that this subject wasn't as important to him as she knew it was.

Evie looked to Ray for support. She honestly didn't know what to say, so she started with the simple stuff.

"I know where to find them if they haven't moved. But you know how territorial wolves are, so I suppose they haven't moved and probably never will," she told him.

"Look, Mom. I didn't ask this to hurt you. I know you don't ever talk about the past, but just recently, the past has come back to bite me on the butt." He chuckled wryly, and she knew he was talking about the fact that she'd never told him he was half-fey. "I think there are a few things I need to know about before any of my missing knowledge

151

inadvertently puts my mate at risk. It's not just me I have to think about anymore, but Deena too. I'd like to know about your old Pack and maybe reach out to them, if they're at all reasonable people."

Evie felt sick. She hadn't been able to talk about the past when she'd thought Ray was gone forever. That included anything about Ray himself and how her family had forbidden her to mate with him. She had kept Josh in the dark about so much. It hadn't really been intentional. It had just been too painful to bring up all those old memories, and they'd done all right on their own. Just the two of them.

But Josh was right. There was more than just the two of them now. Ray was back—a miracle—and Deena was now part of their family. By extension, that meant all those nice people in the minivan, who were out hunting and gathering at the local grocer right now, were also part of it. At a minimum, Josh needed to know the baggage he brought to them, just through his blood.

"The simple truth is…" Ray said, coming to her rescue because Evie couldn't speak around the emotion clogging her throat. "Your mother's Pack forbade her to see me. We eloped. Though at the time, I was in favor of going in and finding out what was wrong with the Pack that they rejected my magic so vehemently. I mean, it's not unheard of for shifters to mate with humans and even fey. It's not like some of the forbidden combinations. There was nothing that should have barred our mating. I would have expected a warm welcome for the increased magic I could bring to the Pack, not the cold reception we got."

"I didn't want you to fight them," Evie said, reaching out to capture her mate's hand with her own. "And it would've come to that, in the end. They weren't listening to me, or to you."

"There was something wrong there, Evie. You must see that now, with the distance of years," Ray insisted.

"Maybe so, but we didn't do anything wrong, and I didn't want you in any danger. You've never seen a wolf Pack when they hunt. Even with all your magic, I feared for your safety," she told him.

Ray moved closer to her, bringing his chair right up against hers before putting his arm around her shoulders. "Sweet Evie." He gave her a rueful grin. "And here, I was imagining all these years that you ran away to protect *them* from *me*."

She chuckled with him, knowing from his teasing tone that he was just joking around, trying to cajole her into a better mood. Ray had always been able to sense when she needed cheering up, though it had to be obvious that talk of her lost Pack would make her feel low.

She felt horrible for the way everything had happened. Had her inability to talk about the past put her son in terrible danger? She feared she knew the answer to that question all too well. Maybe Josh was right. He'd always been brave. Even as a little boy, she'd clung to him. Her anchor in the storm of their lives.

But the storm clouds had finally cleared. Ray was back, and maybe it was about time she faced the fears of the past and put them completely behind her, once and for all. And maybe by coming clean with her son, she could avoid putting him in any more danger from the past rearing its ugly head at the least opportune moment.

"I doubt my parents have ever changed their home phone number," she told Josh. She waited only for him to get a pen and paper before rattling off the digits, and their address, as well. "You should know, your grandfather was the Alpha when I left home, and the Pack was over a hundred strong. Make sure you know what you're doing if you ever decide to enter their territory. My dad's word is law up there, and he didn't like your father at all."

"Yet you raised our son with your family's last name," Ray observed. His voice held a hint of irony, but he didn't seem mad.

"Really?" Josh asked. "I thought you just made up our last name or something. I mean, fey don't have surnames, do they?"

"Surnames in faerie are a bit more complicated than here," Ray explained. "And unless you speak the old tongue, mostly unpronounceable for all except maybe a few of my former Welsh subjects." Ray's tone had gone wry again. "I hear Duncan has affected the surname *le Fey*. Then again, he always enjoyed the region and people of what you now call France." Ray shrugged. "When I lived in Wales, I went by Sir Rayburne of Glyndyfrdwy or just Ray Glyndwr. Of course, it's spelled nothing like it sounds in modern English and would cause more trouble than it's worth to try to stick to the old way. I could probably use something like Glindur here in America, though I suppose that's not a common surname either." Ray seemed to be thinking this through.

"How about Smith?" Evie offered, hoping to make him smile.

He frowned at her, instead. "But I was never a smith. I did not work iron or make horseshoes." He sounded truly insulted, but then, she realized he was teasing her back. "Actually, I've given this some thought. My folk originally hail from the mountains, so Gwyllion might be appropriate. It's the term used for mountain fey in Wales. How'd you like to be Evie Gwyllion rather than Evie Mahigan?"

"Mahigan is just the Cree word for wolf," Josh said quietly. "I looked it up when I was a kid. Not much of a cover, I always thought."

"Well, rightfully, your proper fey name and title is too long to fit on a birth certificate, if modern Americans could even spell it. I'll write it out for you and teach you a bit of the fey language while we're at it, if you wish," Ray offered. "The old tongue will help you channel your magic, so it's something I was going to talk to you about, anyway, but with the wedding, Deena should know more about the fey family she's getting into. She will gain a title by joining our line, though it's only something other fey would recognize. Still, she should be made aware of it, since she knows at least three full-blooded fey at this point, and who knows what the future may bring?"

"I think she'd like that," Josh said, smiling. "Especially since her great-grandmother is going to try to come to officiate at the wedding. Everybody in her family is a bit in awe of Lady Bettina."

"As they should be. A more formidable woman I have never met. She was ancient when I was a lad, and she has served the Goddess for longer than any of us have been alive," Ray revealed.

Silence reigned for a moment while Josh finished his sandwich and then cleared his plate. Evie noticed that he tucked the piece of paper with her parents' address and phone number into his shirt pocket as he rose from the table. She dreaded the phone call she knew he would make. If they rejected her son as they had rejected her and her mate, she would never forgive them.

Evie sent a prayer up to the Mother of All as Josh left the room, saying he wanted to clean up a bit before he rejoined Ray outside for more training. Evie clutched Ray's hand. Josh wasn't fooling anyone. He was going to make that phone call.

"I hope they don't hang up on him," she whispered as Ray's arm tightened around her shoulders.

"If they do, they'll answer to me," he said, a grim look on his face when she turned her head to look at him.

"I wish he'd wait," she whispered, moving her gaze to the archway through which Josh had left.

"He can't. Not with the wedding so close. Now's the time to reach out, if ever there was one. If they want nothing to do with him, better he know that sooner rather than later."

Evie and Ray finished their lunch in silence as she worried about what might be happening in another part of the house where their son was undoubtedly on the phone, calling a certain werewolf household in Canada. She almost wanted to hold her breath until Josh returned, but that was silly. Instead, she held Ray's hand, thoughts racing through her mind about what would happen.

When Josh returned to the kitchen, he was smiling. Just a little, but it was definitely a smile. Evie's worry turned to curiosity in an instant.

"Well?" she prompted when Josh stood for a moment, a bemused expression on his face while he stared out the kitchen window.

He turned toward her. "I'm not sure exactly what just happened, but I spoke to my grandmother. She said she'd call back with their flight information so I could pick them up at the airport tomorrow. They're coming for the wedding."

"They? My mom and dad?" Evie breathed, stunned.

Josh nodded. "And maybe some of the extended family, if they can get away. Mom." Josh's gaze zeroed in on her. "They've been looking for you—for us—for a long time. Grandma said they'd been trying to find you since almost the moment you left home, but your trail was fouled by magic. Once they realized that a mage had interfered, they went on a hunt and found that almost the entire Pack had been under the influence of a human mage with bad intentions. Someone named Bolivar?" Josh's expression turned questioning as Ray tensed beside her.

"I knew it!" Ray exploded up out of his chair, smacking the table as he rose. "I told you there was something wrong with your Pack, Evie."

"The minute you left, Bolivar packed up and moved on, fouling his own trail with magic, as well. He's been in the wind all this time, and they've been searching for you without any luck at all," Josh continued.

Evie felt tears gather. Could it really have been as simple as that? Had she been wrong to leave? She'd thought any wolf who cared enough would've been able to follow her trail. That nobody had come for her had only reinforced her idea that they didn't give a damn about her and wanted no part of a daughter who didn't obey. She'd felt cut off by them, but if what Josh was saying was true—and she had no reason to believe it wasn't—then she'd been wrong. So very wrong.

"I should've let you check, Ray," she whispered, heartbroken at what she had just learned. "My pride got in

156

the way. I thought, when nobody came after me, that they didn't care. That they didn't want me. That they'd shunned me for going against them."

"Sounds like that wasn't what happened at all," Josh said, his voice gentle.

"Foul play," Ray muttered. "That's what happened. That's why they never found you. It was by design, Evie. Designed to destroy you."

"Well, it didn't. I survived and so did Josh," she said, feeling a bit stronger. "I may have been born a Pack animal, but I did pretty well on my own." She stood, trembling with all the revelations.

Josh came over to her and tugged her into his arms. He'd only been a teen when he'd surpassed her height, and he'd enjoyed hugging his *little mama* as he grew into the formidable giant of a man he was today. She'd missed his hugs while he'd been away, searching for answers she hadn't been able to give him.

Come to think of it, she'd survived that too. Maybe her wolf had been a little lonely all this time, but she'd grown stronger for overcoming her fears. She was a survivor, and she was strong. One thing troubled her, though...

"Why target me?" she wondered aloud. "I'm nobody."

It was Ray who replied in a somber tone. "Not true, my love. To me, you are the world." His gaze met hers. "You are the true mate of a fey Knight and the mother of a powerful half-fey werewolf. Cripple you by denying you your Pack, and there is the potential to cripple a strong adversary of darkness—our son, Josh—before he's even born. And it sounds like your disappearance created havoc within your family and Pack. That was probably worth something to this mage, as well."

Josh released her and turned toward Ray. "Grandma said the Pack has been in decline since Mom left. That they could lose her so easily caused chaos within the Pack."

"A strong Pack that had held their lands for generations," Ray commented. "Destroying their cohesiveness could also have been the mage's goal."

One thing was becoming clear to Evie. "We need to know more about this mage."

CHAPTER 19

Deena and her family arrived back at the farm a short while later, and Evie was swept up in the activity of unloading a month's worth of groceries and supplies with everyone else. Deena's mother, Melanie, and her Aunt Gladys were in charge and directed them all like soldiers in a tight-knit unit. Within an hour, everything was in its place, and work had begun in earnest.

The ladies were not only cooking dinner for that night, but also preparing the kitchen for some of the things they'd need to cook in advance for the wedding feast. All sorts of baking was going to start that night and continue on for the next couple of days. Although Evie was a good cook, she'd never done much baking. Even so, she was drafted to help Deena's female relatives, each of whom had been assigned a set of tasks.

Evie didn't mind. In fact, she found she enjoyed working as part of this well-oiled machine. They were a lively bunch with happy attitudes and amusing stories to entertain while they all worked in harmony. Evie felt as if she'd gotten to know Deena's family much better by the time they all turned in that night and was fast on her way to making lasting friendships with them all.

She tumbled into bed that night with Ray, feeling both

happy about the interaction with Deena's family and apprehensive about what might happen tomorrow with her own. Josh had told them over dinner that he'd heard back from his grandmother and that he was going to pick her and his grandfather up from the airport tomorrow morning. That announcement had set off a round of questions for Josh, which he'd answered happily while Evie had sat there, almost shaking at the prospect of seeing her parents again after all this time.

Her inner wolf was both happy and wary. It wanted to see its Pack mates again—especially the Alpha, her sire—but it was afraid of rejection. She'd been rejected before by them. Or, at least, she'd *thought* they'd rejected her all this time. It might take a while before she truly believed their claims, but she was willing to hear them out, for Josh's sake.

Her son seemed so happy at the prospect of completing their little family unit. He tried to hide it, but his mating had changed him. He was no longer the noble lone wolf he'd always tried to be. Then again, except for when his magic emerged and he went off on his own searching for answers, he'd always had Evie. Even if they hadn't lived in the same house since he became an adult, she'd always been nearby. Just a phone call away. She'd been his Pack.

But now that he had Deena and was beginning to experience what it was like to be surrounded by her family, Evie understood why he was asking questions about his own relatives. She just hoped they didn't disappoint him. Evie didn't want to see Josh hurt.

Which was the whole reason she'd stayed away from her family after Ray had disappeared. Oh, she'd thought about crawling back home with her tail tucked between her legs, but she'd never done it. No, her wolf was stronger than that. She might not have been born an Alpha female, but she'd had strength none of them suspected. Not even herself. Until it had come time to rely on it.

She'd raised her son all on her own, and he'd turned out to be a good and honest man. For that, she had absolutely no regrets and would make no apologies.

Ray made love to her gently that night, being as tender as he ever had been with her. Sure enough, his care was exactly what she needed to help her get at least some sleep. Her thoughts had been in a jumble since Josh had broached the subject of his grandparents. The thought that she might be seeing them again for the first time in twenty years the very next morning would overwhelm her if she let it.

Luckily, Ray was there to distract her in the most delightful ways.

She was lying on her side, looking out the window at the silvery stars hanging low in the frosty night air. Ray was spooned around her protectively, and her breath was just returning to normal after one of the mind-shattering orgasms Ray seemed to specialize in. Her thoughts circled back to the coming confrontation.

"Do you think it's really possible that they were looking for me all this time?" Evie asked, not for the first time.

"Yes, I think it's possible. If they were being influenced by a magical outsider, it's more than possible, in fact. It's probable. From just the few details Josh got from your mother, this has every appearance of someone meddling in our affairs for their own evil purposes."

He kept his voice low because the house was still around them, and he probably didn't want to disturb anyone, but there was a decided edge to his tone. He was as angry as she was at the thought that someone could have deliberately interfered with Evie's relationship with her family.

"I don't know what I'm going to say to them," she admitted.

"Start with hello and see how it goes from there," he counseled, squeezing her close, his warm body reassuring to both her human side and her inner wolf. "Don't worry. I'll be right at your side. I'll never leave you again, Evie. You have my word."

It was her turn to soothe him. She turned in his arms and placed gentle kisses all over his face and jaw. "We got through it, Ray. We made it past all the difficulties, and we're together again. Let's not worry about what tomorrow may bring. Just make love to me now and let's focus on each other."

She felt his smile against her lips. "I can definitely do that, my love. In fact, I'm sorry I didn't think of it sooner myself."

She giggled softly and rolled with him as he changed their positions so that he was on top, already joining with her body. She was still wet from their earlier joining, and her body accepted him at once. As if he belonged within her. And he did. He was in her heart. And in her soul. He was her other half. Her mate.

The next morning, Evie woke alone, but she wasn't worried. Ray had gotten into the habit of sneaking out of bed as the first rays of dawn started to lighten the sky. By the time the sun rose, he and Josh were already out in the barnyard, drilling as quietly as they could while Deena greeted her animals and got the farm ready for the morning.

Even with the extra guests in the house, it seemed they were sticking to the same routine. When Evie got up at around eight o'clock, the rest of Deena's family was just starting to get going for the day. Deena's mom and aunt were in the kitchen, making breakfast. Their husbands were helping. Evie offered her assistance but was firmly refused and fussed over, which was an uncommon enough event in her life to make her almost forget about her parents' arrival for a while.

But when Ray came in with Deena and joined her at the table with the other two couples, *sans* Josh, Evie realized their son must have already left for the airport. It wasn't a quick trip, so she had an hour or two before he'd be back with her parents.

They'd discussed it last night, and Evie was happy to let Josh meet them first. They had no history with him, so perhaps they could form some kind of bond without her influence. And putting off the uncomfortable encounter as long as possible might be cowardly, but right now, that strategy suited Evie just fine.

Ray sat beside her with a plate full of scrambled eggs and bacon. Evie had already finished her own breakfast, but she was enjoying a cup of coffee with everyone as they sat around and talked about the upcoming wedding.

Melanie and Gladys had big plans for cooking and cleaning, even though Evie knew Deena and Josh had already spent a lot of time cleaning the house and moving things around in preparation for their guests. This was an industrious group of people, and they didn't just sit around waiting for things to happen, it seemed.

They were doers. Evie liked that about them. They all seemed to have very positive attitudes and were eager to accept Josh into the family. As far as Evie was concerned, that was the golden ticket. If they loved and accepted Josh, then she would love and accept them. The fact that they were all pretty decent people made it all that much easier.

While Ray was eating and the conversation flowed around them, Evie sipped coffee. She'd almost settled her nerves when her superior werewolf hearing told her someone was driving up the gravel driveway. Josh. And her parents? No. She wasn't ready!

Ray put a hand out and grasped hers, catching her attention. "It'll be all right, no matter what," he whispered, reassuring her.

Deena had stood even before Evie heard the telltale sounds. Of course. She'd felt the vehicle pass over her wards on the property. Evie hadn't really known about such things before the whole incident in North Dakota, but she realized how handy it must be to have early warning about visitors. Deena had known of their arrival even before Evie, which wasn't something Evie was used to. Usually, her shifter senses put her one step ahead of everyone else.

"They're here," Deena told everyone before leaving the kitchen and heading for the front door. She was going to greet them, as was only proper. It was her house, after all.

Evie felt a knot of dread form in her stomach. There was also a little ray of hope trying to break through, but it was having a hard time getting past all the hurt and sadness and fear.

"We'll all stay here for now," Melanie told her in a gentle voice. "You probably need some time together first to square things. I hope you don't mind, but Deena told us a little bit about what happened."

"I don't mind," Evie told the other woman, glad she wouldn't have to explain the dynamics of what was about to happen. "Thanks for understanding."

Evie took a deep breath and pushed back from the table. She stood with Ray beside her. He was in this with her, which was a tremendous help. She grabbed onto his hand as they walked out of the kitchen and headed for whatever reaction her family might have.

She knew one thing. If they still objected to Ray, then she didn't need them in her life. If, however, they were willing to accept her mate, then she'd give them a chance. She wanted to hear the explanations from them directly. She knew what they'd told Josh over the phone, but she needed to hear it in person, from them, to judge for herself whether or not it was true.

Ray's presence at her side was reassuring as they crossed the house toward the front door. As she passed the window, Evie could just make out a small group of people standing in the drive, next to a couple of suitcases. Josh and Deena stood with their backs to the house, partially blocking the view of the newcomers, but Evie thought she caught a glimpse of her mother's hair—now just a little gray around the temples. Her breath caught as she paused at the door. Could she really do this?

The choice was taken out of her hands when Ray opened the door, and everyone turned to look at her. Josh and Deena were smiling encouragingly, and then, Evie saw her mother and father for the first time in so very, very long...

Time stopped. Everyone stood still for a moment as Evie

and her parents just looked at each other.

Then, Evie noticed the tears on her mother's face, and she started moving again. Step by step, she walked closer to where her mother and father waited. She passed Josh, reaching out to touch his arm as she went, then stood face to face with her mother.

"Hi, Mom," Evie found herself saying.

The moment was surreal. She hadn't ever imagined talking to her mother again. At least not in this lifetime. She'd thought she'd been written off. Shunned. Forgotten.

If she'd been a good little loyal Pack wolf, she probably should have greeted the Alpha male first, but this was her family. Things were a little different within the family unit. Sure, her father had been the one to forbid her relationship with Ray, but the part that had hurt the most was her mother's silence.

Evie was used to her father—the big Alpha male of the entire Pack—making decrees she didn't always agree with, but her mother's betrayal had been the worst part. Of course, they were denying it all, claiming they were under the influence of some kind of evil magic.

Easy enough to say. Hard to prove, this late in the game. Ever since Josh had told her about the supposed mage, Evie had been turning the story over in her mind. Frankly, she was on the fence. Torn between wanting to believe that her family had never really abandoned her and wanting to carry the grudge that had built up in her mind and heart over the many years when she'd needed them and they hadn't been there.

"Oh, Evie..." Her mother broke into tears, crying hard now.

Evie's first impulse was to comfort, but there were too many questions between them still. She held back, turning, instead, to look at her father. The Alpha wolf.

"I'm sorry, munchkin," he said in a soft voice, filled with regret.

The childhood nickname was like a gut punch. And the apology was unprecedented. Never had Evie heard Alpha

Mahigan apologize to anyone for anything. That he was doing so now meant something significant.

"Hi, Dad." It was all she could think of to say at the moment. Evie's mind was in chaos. Was this the homecoming she'd hoped for? She still wasn't sure.

"Evie, I want you to know, we searched for you," her father said in that strong voice she remembered so well. "We've *been* searching for you the last twenty years. Josh, here, has told us a bit about where you've been and what happened between you and your mate, and I can't tell you how sorry I am that you thought you weren't welcome back home. You were always welcome. You *are* always welcome. I still consider you part of the Pack, and if you want it, your place has been kept open for you."

"My place? As what? I was a submissive female when I left. I knew that always disappointed you, but I was what I was. I couldn't change that unless I changed on a fundamental level." She shrugged. It might be painful to discuss these matters, but it was very necessary that they understand she was no longer the girl that they had known. "And I did change. These years on my own with Josh...they changed me."

"Maybe so," her father admitted. "But you'll always be my daughter. That's your place in the Pack. If you want it."

Evie was stunned, but also wary. "I might have to get back to you on that," she told him, surprised to see sadness and a bit of disappointment in his eyes. "Ray is back now," she declared, taking Ray's hand as he came to stand at her side. "He's my mate, and nothing will ever change that."

The Alpha nodded. "I understand." Her father reached out to shake Ray's right hand in a respectful manner.

Well, that was new. Her dad had never been willing to give Ray the time of day all those years ago. In fact, he'd forbidden Ray to come anywhere near Pack territory. Evie had had to sneak out to see him the few times they'd dated before Ray had asked her to be his wife.

Evie had known from the first time she saw Ray in town

that he was something special to her. She'd gone against her family—against her Alpha—to see Ray because her inner wolf knew her mate when she saw him. It had taken only a few dates for Ray to propose, and then, Evie had tried to get approval from her father, but he'd gone into a rage.

She'd run away that night and never looked back. She and Ray had left the territory and struck out on their own. They'd spent a glorious few months together as newlyweds. They'd fixed up the cabin in the middle of North Dakota, far from her Canadian homeland, and made a home for themselves.

Then, Ray had disappeared. And then, Evie realized she was pregnant. A lot had happened in a short space of time all those years ago, culminating in Evie being left on her own with the baby to raise all by herself.

"Evie, honey..." Her mother had gotten control over her emotions somewhat. "Can you forgive me? I should've said something. I should've done more. I had no idea you would run away like that. I doubted your fey mate's sincerity, and I'm so sorry." Tears punctuated each of her mother's words.

Evie didn't know what to think. Those empty years where the only joy in her life had been her son weighed heavily.

"You forgave me," Ray reminded her, whispering near her ear.

And he was right. She'd forgiven him almost immediately. She hadn't been suspicious of his tale of imprisonment in the fey realm. She'd given him the benefit of the doubt.

She should probably do the same for her parents. Plus, there was Josh to consider. And now, Deena. They would want to know Evie's family and had every right to learn more about the Pack Evie had grown up in.

All at once, the tension in her spine eased, and she walked into her mother's arms.

"There's nothing to forgive," she told her mother, as she'd earlier told Ray.

It wasn't healthy to keep grudges. She was through with all that. This moment marked a new beginning for her and her family. All of them. Ray, Josh, her parents, Deena and her family. They were all starting over as of now.

CHAPTER 20

Evie was floored by the outpouring of love from her mother and father. She hadn't expected it, but she could feel it in their embrace. They just stood there, on the gravel drive, hugging for long moments, their inner wolves basking in the reunion with their family. Their Pack.

Josh came over and joined the huddle. Evie had started out by hugging her mother, but her father had joined them, wrapping his arms around the two women from the side and bowing his head over them. Josh took up the same pose on the other side, and they all just stood there for a moment. Then, Josh stepped back first.

"I think we should all go for a run," he said, surprising her. Josh had seemed more fey than wolf these past days, but around Pack, maybe his wolf was reasserting itself.

"We should," Evie's father agreed, "but first, we should greet Deena's family properly. It would be rude not to say hello. We can run tonight, if there's no objection."

When the humans and fey were asleep, her father meant. That got through to Evie, and she finally stepped back from her mother. "Dad's right. You need to meet Deena's family. They're really great."

Evie turned toward the house, and just like that, Deena's folks opened the door, as if they'd been watching and waiting for their turn. Josh got the bags, gesturing for his grandfather and Ray to go ahead with the women.

Evie started walking but slowed when she realized her father and Ray had stopped to face each other. She listened eagerly, afraid some sort of confrontation was in the works. What she heard instead was a balm to her battered heart.

Her father held out his hand again to Ray. "I only met you the once, Sir Rayburne, and I have to admit, I misjudged you. I didn't think a fey could form a serious bond with one of our kind, but you proved me wrong. I hope you'll accept my apology, as well."

"As my mate said…" Ray glanced at her and smiled that smile that was just for her. Then, he turned back to her dad and took his hand in a strong grip. "There is nothing to forgive." They shook hands and both smiled. When the handshake was over, Ray turned, and they caught up with her, walking the short distance to the house. "I would like to ask you a bit about this Bolivar, when we have a few minutes. A threat like that shouldn't be left walking."

Her dad growled. "We've been looking for him as long as we've been looking for Evie. Dead end after dead end is all we've found, but our Margo has a complete file on all the information we've managed to turn up. I'll call her and ask her to bring the information with her."

Evie remembered a young cousin named Margo, but she'd been just a toddler when Evie had left. Then, her father's words got through. "Wait, Margo's coming here?"

"Josh invited the whole Pack to his wedding. A bunch of them are loading up their trailers and will be heading down here in a few days. Your mother already scoped out a local campground and got the owner to open it up special just for us over the holidays."

"You're joking." Evie was floored. The whole Pack had been mobilized? Did Josh really understand what that would mean?

Her father just laughed. "Don't worry. Young Josh will be okay. He's an Alpha if I ever met one. Nobody in the Pack can touch him."

"He's half-fey," Ray reminded him. "I don't expect any wolf Packs to accept an Alpha with his kind of magic."

"They don't have to accept him as *their* Alpha. Just as *an* Alpha. I'm still in charge of the Pack, and I have a successor already picked out that the Pack accepts and respects. But every one of us has a place in the dominance chain. I suspect my Evie has risen to a much stronger position through her hardships, and Josh will have a place near the top, if I'm any judge. Which means nobody will pick on him or criticize his mate. Alphas—whether the Alpha of a small family group or Alpha of the whole damned Pack—don't take crap from anybody."

Evie's mother was the first to reach the door, and she was welcomed by Deena's parents. They were all smiles, and the ladies exchanged kisses on the cheek.

"I'm Jaquelyn, Josh's grandmother. Call me Jacki," Evie heard her mom tell Melanie. It sounded strange to hear anybody claim Josh as anything other than Evie's son. She realized she'd better learn to share. Josh had a family now. Not just Evie's family, but Deena's, as well.

"And I'm Tom Mahigan," Evie's dad said, reaching out to shake hands with Deena's folks, as friendly and polite as Evie had ever seen him.

Perhaps he'd mellowed with age. Evie knew she wasn't the same callow youth who had crept away from home in the middle of the night all those years ago. She shouldn't expect that her family hadn't changed in the intervening years either.

No doubt about it. This was going to be a big adjustment.

"It good to meet you, Alpha Mahigan," Deena's father said, surprising Evie with his knowledge of werewolf etiquette. Peter was a human mage, after all. Nobody expected him to know the proper terms of address or titles, yet he'd just proven them wrong.

Deena's dad stood tall and silent while the Alpha appraised him, then the Alpha grinned. "You may or may not realize this, but by mating my grandson, your daughter just made you members of my extended family, which for us, is the Pack. Welcome to the Stony Ridge Pack."

"Really?" Deena seemed to be trying to suppress a giggle. *Uh-oh.*

"Why? What is it?" Evie asked gently, trying to avert an incident.

"Well, it's just that there's a retirement home by that name a few miles east on the county road. Somehow, I don't think the gray-haired little old ladies that live there are affiliated with you guys." Deena did laugh this time, but it was humor shared by all.

"I'd have to check to be absolutely certain," Tom said, scratching his head comically, "but I think it's safe to assume they're not affiliated with our Pack."

The next couple of days saw an influx of Stony Ridge Pack members into the tiny town in rural Pennsylvania. They essentially took over a campground that had been closed for the season until Jacki got hold of the owner and basically made him an offer he couldn't refuse. Not that she threatened the man in any way. More like she cut a deal that compensated him handsomely for allowing her family to use his land, with the promise that they would leave it exactly as they had found it—completely winterized and ready for the cold season ahead.

They'd also agreed to do a few needed repairs while they were there. So actually, they were leaving the place better than they had found it. The owner would be happy with his pristine facilities, and he would have extra income during the lean winter months. And the werewolf Pack was thrilled with a quiet, private, large wooded space in which to park their trailers and let their wolves run free. Win-win for all concerned.

For Evie, each new relative or childhood friend's arrival was an unbelievable blessing. Not just her immediate family had made the long trip, but pretty much every member of the Pack who was physically able to come. She greeted each one with happy tears and a feeling of overwhelming joy. And person by person, it began to sink in. They really hadn't shunned her for mating outside their species. They hadn't wanted her to go, and they really had been looking for her all this time.

In fact, her cousin, Margo, whom she remembered only as a chubby toddler, was now a grown woman who had taken the ongoing search for not only Evie but also for the enemy, Bolivar, and made a profession out of it. She was employed as a private investigator, working with the premier shifter PI firm in North America. In fact, she was head of the Canadian branch of the detective agency owned by Collin Hastings, a hawk shifter who specialized in helping other magical folk with investigations.

The Pack seemed to really accept Deena's family, as well, and got into the spirit of decorating and preparing for the wedding as if they'd always been part of it. The guest list had effectively tripled with the addition of the Pack, but so had the manpower.

The ceremony was still to be held in the circle of stones, but now, the after-party was going to range from the house out into the woods, the barn, and even the fields. The Pack liked parties and would attend in both human and wolf form, depending on their mood. Shifters rarely felt the cold, so the outdoors, even on the Winter Solstice, was fine for them. The humans and priestesses would spend most of their time in the house since they were more susceptible to the cold, but the shifters would range in and out of the large farmhouse, making sure to mingle with the new members of the extended Pack.

It was really amazing to Evie how well they were all working together. It was also amazing how easily they accepted not only Josh, but Ray and the human mages who were part of Deena's family. Perhaps her Pack wasn't as closed-minded as she'd thought.

She realized she'd been wrong about a lot of things where the Pack was concerned, and over those few days between

BIANCA D'ARC

their arrival and the wedding, she spent time with each member of the Pack, reaffirming the bonds that should never have been broken. She spent a lot of time with her mother, in particular, and learned a great deal about the Pack's sworn enemy, a mage named Bolivar.

Evie didn't really remember much about him from those last few days she'd spent among the Pack. Her mind had been full of Ray back then and her own problems. She vaguely recalled a man who had lived on the outskirts of the nearby town. His car had broken down on Pack lands, and her father had helped him.

Had that been the moment when Bolivar first tried to influence her Pack against her? They spent more than a few conversations trying to figure that one out. Whatever the exact sequence of events had been, it was now clear that Bolivar *had* been influencing more than one member of the Pack. Evie's father had been the most damaging connection, of course. If evil tainted the Alpha, it spread throughout the Pack like wildfire.

Which was exactly what had happened. The bonds of family and friendship that had held the Pack together for so long had been damaged and disrupted by outside magic. If not for that, Evie never would have been able to leave so easily, or be lost so completely.

"I've almost had him a few different times," Margo told Evie one night as they discussed the Bolivar problem once more after a sumptuous dinner.

The old farmhouse was filled to capacity, and every night was like a party in itself as different groups formed in the living room, kitchen, even the laundry room, to talk and just be near each other after dinner. The majority of the Pack would drive back to the campground later that night, but a few always remained in wolf form, prowling the perimeter with Deena and Josh's permission and thanks. While the Pack was here, it would protect its own. The message was clear and quite unexpected, though much appreciated.

"Let me guess," Ray said, not unkindly, in response to

174

Margo's words. "Bolivar is always one step ahead."

Margo let out a frustrated growl that was answer enough, but she went on to explain. "Always. He always seems to know when I'm closing in and high-tails it just before I can get to him."

"I wouldn't be surprised if one of his gifts is clairvoyance," Ray observed.

"Huh." Margo slouched in her seat, a bit deflated. "I hadn't considered that, though I guess I should have. I just thought he had better intel than I do."

"He might have that, as well," Ray agreed. "But he's a mage. Mages have all sorts of different powers that could interfere with your investigative methods."

"What you need is another mage," Gabe volunteered. Evie had noticed the way Gabe's eyes followed Margo around when the younger woman wasn't looking. Deena's brother seemed to always be wherever Margo was, and so far, the young werewolf woman hadn't seemed to notice. At least not overtly. "Takes a mage to catch a mage," Gabe went on, nodding.

"He could be right," Ray offered, tilting his head as if considering the younger man's words. "The right kind of spell could block Bolivar's clairvoyance—if he has any. Then, you could get closer to him without his knowledge. As long as he doesn't also have mundane methods of knowing your movements."

Margo looked pensive, as if considering his words. "So, a private operation. No backup. No support. No communications with anyone outside the team that goes in to catch Bolivar."

"And preferably as small a team as possible," Ray agreed, clearly getting into the spirit of a planning session as he leaned forward in his chair. "A mage, for sure. With the right kind of skills. A good knowledge of spell work is essential. He's a good choice." Ray gestured to Gabe then looked back at Margo. "And you, if this is what you really want to do. The two of you could probably take Bolivar down on your own, if you worked together. Or at least get close enough to trap him then call for reinforcements."

Margo looked surprised, shooting a questioning glance at Gabe and then looking back at Ray. "Does he have the right kind of knowledge?"

Margo looked as if she wanted to ask more but was holding her tongue for some reason. Evie wanted to grin. It was clear now to Evie, at least, that Margo had some kind of strong opinion about Gabe, but she was playing her cards close to her chest.

"Uncle Geoff is the premier spell casting teacher in our region, and I've been learning from him since I was a kid," Gabe proclaimed. "And my dad taught me pretty much everything he knows about potions."

"And let's not forget your fey heritage," Ray put in. "You've got more power—and of a different flavor—than human mages. If Bolivar is wholly human, you'd likely easily overpower him. If he's something more, then so are you. And you'd have werewolf backup. Between the two of you, and the element of surprise, I think you'd be able to take him down."

Margo sat back with a lurch. Her expression was a little lost for a moment before she regained her composure. Evie thought she recognized the look of a person who knew they were fighting fate.

CHAPTER 21

By the time the day of the winter solstice arrived, everyone had arrived in Pennsylvania, except for one last final person. Perhaps the most important person, aside from the bride and groom. The officiant had yet to make her appearance. The High Priestess Bettina, councilor to the Lords of all were and great-grandmother many times removed of the bride's matriarchal line.

Ray wasn't too concerned. Like him, Bettina was fully fey. She could port from place to place easily, and considering she had spent the last century or two, to his knowledge, in the mortal realm, she probably could do it with more finesse than any other fey he knew. Still, he figured she would use the standing stones to camouflage and contain the energy of her port.

Which was why he'd decided to keep watch from outside the circle. He wanted a chance to reacquaint himself with her privately, before the rest of the family became aware of her presence.

Sure enough, a couple of hours after lunch, Bettina arrived. Ray saw the flash of multicolored light from within the stone circle, but even though he was looking for it, he didn't feel the telltale ripple of magic. Her port was near perfection, creating very little disturbance in the surrounding energies. He'd have to ask her for pointers, since he intended on staying in this realm for many years to come.

She turned within the circle and saw him, a smile lighting her petite face.

"Rayburne, it is good to see you again. I had feared the worst when you went missing." Bettina walked over to him, stepping lightly out of the protection of the circle to face him.

"Lady Bettina," Ray said with more formality. She was his elder, though she didn't really look it, and his superior in magic, as well. Bettina was one of the most powerful fey ever to choose the mortal realm over faerie. He bowed his head to her in respect. "You look as lovely as ever, and your magical skill is even more impressive than I remember. Your port here was flawless."

Bettina smiled up at him. "I've had a lot of practice. Especially with this particular set of standing stones. Deena is one of my favorites, you know." Bettina winked as they turned and began walking through the woods at a sedate pace, making their way toward the house in the distance.

"I didn't quite realize that, but I can see why. She is lovely and a perfect match for my son," Ray admitted. "I still can't quite believe I even have a son, much less one who is a fully grown and powerful warrior."

"You missed a lot," Bettina said softly, putting one hand on his forearm.

Even such a light touch let him feel the enormity of her power as their magics met and clashed just the tiniest bit. Nothing harmful. Just the meeting to two energies that were slightly out of synch with each other.

"I did," he agreed, sighing because he could do nothing about the past now.

"You don't sound bitter," she remarked quietly. "That's good. Even *our* lives are too short to waste much time on bitterness."

"Just being back together with Evie has gone a long way toward resolving my feelings on the issue. I regret the wasted time, and missing out on Josh's youth, but I'm grateful to be here now with them both."

"It is a healthy attitude," Bettina complimented him. "And you are looking well after your ordeal. I understand you've been given the task of training your son in the ways of Knighthood."

It wasn't phrased as a question, but he knew it was one, nevertheless.

"Indeed I have. Josh is going to be a magnificent addition to our Order, and I don't say that just because he's my son. His wolf instincts and fey power work together to give him an edge that most of my brethren lack." Ray could go on and on about Josh's agility and quick mind, but he didn't want to sound like a braggart.

"You haven't been back very long, but you should know that more and more mixed matings and hybrid children have been appearing over the past two decades. I've not seen anything like it since the time of the Destroyer, and frankly, it has me very concerned," she admitted. "There are also unconfirmed reports that Elspeth might already have returned to this realm. If so, she's lying low for now. No doubt it would have been very taxing to her own personal power to cross such a great divide between the forgotten realm into which she was cast and this one. Perhaps she is recovering. If that's the case, then our time for preparation grows short."

Ray frowned. "You really think she could already be here?"

Bettina paused and turned to look at him. "I'm not sure, but there are grave signs all over the globe. We already have confirmation that the leviathan is menacing a town made up of mostly bear shifters in the Pacific Northwest. If the leviathan is here, then someone must have summoned it. It is not a creature of this realm. It does not belong here and could not have come here on its own to prey upon magical folk. If they managed to summon it, they might also have figured out how to open the portal into the farthest realms."

"This is grim news, indeed," Ray replied, his mind already

working on what they would have to do to prepare. He fully intended to accelerate Josh's training. No way would he let his only son go out to meet such evil unprepared.

"Indeed," Bettina agreed, but then, she seemed to shake off her serious demeanor. "But thankfully, today, we can put that aside for now and concentrate on the joyful festivities to come. I never expected that our families would combine in this way, but I can't say I mind. You have always proven to be a man of great integrity. If your son is half the man you are, my granddaughter will live a blessed life with him."

"I'm honored you would say so," Ray told her as they broke out of the woods and into the clearing where various members of the two families were setting up picnic tables and chairs.

It was cold out, but the werewolves didn't mind a little chilly weather, and Deena's somewhat more fragile relatives were bundled up in winter coats, hats, scarves and gloves. They all looked like they were having a fun time decorating the backyard. But when they caught sight of Bettina, a hush came over the previously boisterous gathering.

It was Gabe who defied convention and came over to them, lifting Bettina right off her feet and hugging her as he grinned happily. "Grandma! It's been too long." He placed a smacking kiss on her cheek as he set the High Priestess back down on the ground.

Everybody seemed to be holding their breath. The wolves, in particular, were waiting to see what the all-powerful High Priestess would do to the young scamp who dared behave so familiarly.

"Gabriel!" Bettina called out loudly. "You haven't changed a bit." She winked at him and smiled. "That's good. Don't ever change," she stage-whispered, at which point the avidly-watching werewolves all breathed a collective sigh of relief.

The rest of Deena's family came out to greet Bettina, and then, it was time to introduce the Stony Ridge Pack to Deena's rather formidable great-grandmother. Josh and Deena were around the front of the house, so as it happened, they were among the last to greet the High Priestess.

Deena, of course, gave her great-grandmother an uninhibited hug. It was clear the two women were very close, even though many years and a vast difference in experience existed between them. Still, they appeared to have more in common than not, and there was a very obvious bond of love between them. It was clear Bettina took a deep interest those of her family line.

Ray watched closely as Bettina met Josh for the first time. Would the High Priestess give his son a hard time? If so, what could he possibly do about it besides just be a reassuring presence watching over him from the sidelines? Perhaps that was enough. Perhaps it was just good for Josh to see his family there, observing and supporting.

That was probably a novel enough experience for him, considering he'd grown up with only his mother for support. Now, he had Ray and an entire wolf Pack to watch his back. Perhaps Josh didn't need their help, but it probably still meant something to him to know it was available.

Regardless, Ray needn't have worried. Bettina greeted Josh with a wide smile and a big hug.

"It's so good to meet you," Bettina said as she drew back from the embrace. "I've never seen my Deena so happy before, and I think that's down to you, young man. I'm so glad you've found each other."

"I am too, milady," Josh said quietly, returning her smile as Deena snuggled into his side, his arm around her shoulders.

"Now then." Bettina clapped her hands together, smiling brightly. "We'll do the ceremony at moonrise, in conjunction with the solstice celebration. We'll do the rituals, and then, it'll be time to party."

A little cheer went up from all those who had gathered around to unabashedly listen in. What looked like nearly the whole Pack was watching and almost all of Deena's relatives too. They'd crept in from all directions while Ray had been intent upon the first contact between his son and the High

Priestess. Those wolves were silent, but the humans hadn't done too bad either. Ray had barely noticed their arrival.

Evie sniffled at the ceremony. She couldn't help it and felt a kinship with Deena's mother and aunt, who were sniffling right along with her, even as they assisted the High Priestess with the rest of the ritual. Not only were they calling down the blessings of the Goddess on the newly mated pair, but they were raising prayers to the heavens in celebration of the solstice. The time when the sun was at its weakest point and it made the turn to start growing stronger again.

Little by little, each day now, the days would get longer and longer until they reached Midsummer, six months away. Even though winter was only really just starting in this hemisphere, it was a time of joy and rebirth. A time of increase. Of restoration.

It was an auspicious time to celebrate Josh and Deena's mating.

As the High Priestess called Josh and Deena forward, magic started to visibly shimmer inside the stone circle. Since the circle was small, compared to the much larger stones in North Dakota, most of the Pack and Deena's extended family was outside, looking in. There was only room enough for Deena's parents, Ray, Evie, Josh's grandparents, and Deena's aunt and uncle.

Duncan had shown up right before the ceremony was to begin, much to Evie's surprise, and evened up the numbers. Even more intriguing, he stood with Bettina by the altar, facing Josh and Deena. The remaining four couples ranged along the cardinal points within the circle.

It was clear to Evie that Bettina and Duncan knew each other well. There was a mutual respect easily visible between them as they worked together, Duncan acting as sort of an acolyte, assisting Bettina with the water, fire, earth and air symbols needed for the ceremony.

Evie watched in awe as she saw a true manifestation of magic within that small stone circle. She'd attended such rituals before, but seldom had she encountered so much power in such a small space.

As Bettina called down the blessings of the Goddess, certain people within the circle began to glow. The three Knights were revealed first, Duncan and Ray wearing glowing golden armor as they stood respectfully. Josh's armor was made of pure white light, different but still as powerful and luminous as the others.

That settled that question, then. The Goddess had decided to reveal the status of all three men as Her Knights to everyone gathered here tonight. Evie would worry about what that might mean for the future later.

For now, the spectacle was breathtaking. Bettina glowed, as well, with a special iridescence that was unlike anything else within the circle or without. Evie thought she even saw a hint of gossamer wings behind the ancient fey priestess, but she couldn't be absolutely certain. Deena glowed with the purity of her spirit, as did her mother and aunt. Deena's glow was white and sparkly, like her mate's. Her mother and aunt showed that same slightly golden hue of the two older Knights.

Deena's father and uncle showed only sparks of energy swirling around them in subdued shades of blue, some kind of reflection of their personal magic. Evie looked down and realized she too had a slight glow of golden brown and forest green. The colors of the earth magic that was part of her soul, she knew.

Evie was entranced by the intensity of the magic that had gathered here this night. She was so happy for Josh and Deena, to have their mating celebrated in such a way. Nobody had done anything like this for Evie and Ray. Perhaps if they'd had the support of their families and friends, they would've had an easier life. But Evie was just glad to have him here with her now. She counted herself blessed to have him back in her life, no matter what.

When the ritual had turned from the acknowledgment of Josh and Deena's new bond to the celebration of the solstice,

Evie reached up to wipe away the single tear that had escaped her control. Ray took hold of her other hand, squeezing it gently, reassuringly. She looked up at him and was lost for a moment in the beauty of his eyes surrounded by the golden glow of his magical armor.

When she heard the High Priestess say her name, Evie was caught off guard. She turned to find everyone looking at her and Ray, encouraging smiles on all faces. What had she missed?

"I asked Lady Bettina to say a few words for us," Ray told her in a whisper only she could hear. "Words that should have been said decades ago and acknowledged by your Pack." He leaned down to place a soft kiss on her forehead. "I didn't want to steal any of Josh and Deena's thunder, but this opportunity was too good to pass up. Who knows when we'll see the High Priestess again and have all our friends here to witness it?"

Evie's heart melted right there on the spot.

As she walked toward the altar with Ray holding her hand, she let the tears fall this time, knowing it would be useless to try to stop them. They were tears of happiness. Tears of emotion, because her mate had touched a deep part of her inner being that had needed this public acknowledgment in front of all their friends and family.

With Josh and Deena standing beside them and the entire Stony Ridge Pack looking on in approval, the High Priestess spoke powerful blessings over their mating and the renewal of their commitment to each other. When it was done, the Pack sent up a howl sure to startle every neighbor within earshot. Deena might have to field a few questions come the morning about the wolf Pack, but Evie didn't let that stop her from enjoying the moment.

CHAPTER 22

The party afterward was focused on Josh and Deena, as it should be, but Evie was gratified by the number of folks who came by to offer their good wishes to her and Ray, as well. And the new respect she saw in her Pack members' eyes for Ray, Josh, and even Duncan, was good to see. A few of the braver men asked Ray about being a Knight, and Evie loved the fact that he could hold his head up and let them all see what made him so special.

Of course, they should've trusted her instincts all those years ago on that score, but Evie was coming to believe that they'd been under an evil influence. They were so different now from the way they'd been those last few weeks while she'd still been at home. There had definitely been some kind of dark cloud over her Pack back then. It was good to see them back to the way things should have been all along. It was just a shame it had taken so long to get to this point.

"This is a party," a musical female voice said from right beside Evie. "No place for deep thoughts." Startled, Evie discovered the High Priestess had somehow snuck up on her.

"Caught me." Evie shook her head. "Thanks for what you did for me and Ray."

"No thanks necessary," Bettina said, gesturing with her hand in a finishing motion. "Ray was right to ask for the recognition of your mating, and I'm glad I could be the one to do it. You've raised a fine son, who has now joined your line to mine, and I couldn't be happier."

"I'm thrilled on all counts. Deena is a beautiful soul, and she's good for Josh," Evie agreed, watching the newlyweds holding court a few yards away. Everyone was happy, and food and drink were flowing from the house out into the backyard party for the heartier souls and those whose inner magic kept them warm. "We're going to get a house nearby so Ray can be around to teach Josh about his new calling," Evie told Bettina.

"That's good. Josh will need his father as never before now that he's a Knight. You raised him well, and he's a strong, pure-hearted man, but he needs skills only his father can teach him. I think he'd like to have you around too, though." Bettina grinned as she said the words. "Men don't like to admit it, but even when they're grown, they still need their mothers from time to time. Even if they have a mate."

Evie laughed. "He won't hear it from me, but I think you're right."

Ray returned to her side at that moment, having stepped away to refresh their drinks and get a plate of snacks. He handed Evie her glass and offered his politely to Bettina, but the High Priestess declined. She did take one of the cookies that were on the plate, though, biting into it with a comically greedy expression.

"Don't mind me, but I absolutely adore these cookies that Gladys makes. They're half the reason I attend as many family gatherings as I can manage."

"What's the other half?" Evie asked, half-joking and half-curious.

Bettina sobered, her eyes going soft as she looked around at her family. "When you've lived as long as I have, it's good to reinforce the connections with the living family I have left. It's too easy to dwell on those who have moved on. And those who I am unable to commune with here in the mortal realm."

"You lost your mate," Evie realized, though it was the only thing that made sense. Bettina had relatives, but no mate. She must've lost her husband long ago.

"He wasn't my mate in the sense that your people understand," Bettina told her candidly. "But I did love him. Leyland was a human mage of great power and a handsome devil to boot. We came together only briefly centuries before the great war. I was spending time between realms, and my daughter, Larissa, was born and raised mostly in faerie, though she was half-human. She eventually found a mate here in the mortal realm, and I decided to spend more time here to be with her and watch over her family as it grew. Then, the Destroyer raised her ugly head, and Larissa and her mate were killed in the fighting. I protected their children as best I could until we were able to defeat Elspeth. Ever since that time, I've watched over Larissa's children's children, and watched the line ebb and flow."

Evie's heart went out to the High Priestess, realizing, for perhaps the first time, that Bettina had to have seen a lot of loss over her many years. What a sad existence. Evie dared greatly, reaching out to put her arm around Bettina's shoulders.

"Your granddaughter will be safe with my son. Or, at least as safe as it's possible to be with the renewed tensions in the world today."

Bettina accepted the comfort Evie offered, and they stood together for a moment, Bettina's hand rising to touch Evie's hand that was on her shoulder. It was a moment of connection between two Alpha females who cared greatly for their children.

"It's good that you realize our times will not be easy from here on out," Bettina told her as the moment ended and Evie moved away. "All the signs I'm seeing point to the fact that you and your mate, along with the many other newly-formed inter-species matings and hybrid children, will have a role to play if the Destroyer returns. Your job now it to prepare as best you can."

Evie looked deep into Bettina's serious eyes. "I'll do all in my power to do so and to help the rest of the family do the same. We're all connected now," Evie reminded the High Priestess. "I'll do my best by your blood as I would my own."

"That's all I can ask, and more than I'd hoped for," Bettina replied, smiling softly as she put her hands on Evie's shoulders, as if in benediction.

Ray had been occupied during this conversation, talking with Duncan, who stood at his side. Bettina left Evie a few moments later and made the rounds, talking to everyone for a minute or two before she quietly left, heading back to the stone circle. When she ported out of Pennsylvania, nobody noticed, except maybe those who already missed her comforting presence.

It was a few hours later when Ray and Evie were sitting together, under the stars. Neither of them were affected that badly by the cold, and the night was crisp and clear. Millions of stars twinkled down on them, and most of the wolf Pack had claimed comfy spots around the backyard. A few of the Deena's younger relatives had built a fire in the barbeque pit and were toasting marshmallows and telling stories.

The party was winding down a bit for the moment, though the wolves would be running over the fields later that night, for sure. Josh and Evie would be running with them while Ray and Deena held down the fort—or, rather, the farm.

For now, though, everyone was enjoying a few quiet moments after eating the huge meal Deena's mother and aunt had organized. The food had been plentiful and delicious, and the sister priestesses were heaped with praise for their part in a lovely evening.

Seeing how happy Josh and Deena were together was a blessing. Evie couldn't help smiling every time she caught them gazing at each other with that tender expression on both their faces. Young love was beautiful to behold.

More seasoned love wasn't bad either, she thought, feeling Ray's arms come around her as he shifted to sit behind her on the blanket he'd spread over the grass for her comfort. Then again, she felt a bit like a newlywed. They hadn't seen each other for twenty years, and before that, they'd only been together as mates for a few months. So, maybe they were getting a second chance at a honeymoon.

"When do you want to start looking at houses?" Evie asked Ray out of the blue.

He didn't miss a beat. "How about tomorrow afternoon? I picked up a newspaper during one of the shopping runs and circled a few likely ads for real estate agents."

She turned to smile up at him. "I love that about you. Always thinking a few steps ahead."

"I have to if I'm going to keep up with my quick-witted, sexy werewolf mate." He leaned in and nipped her ear playfully. "Are you sure you don't mind moving?"

"I love you, Ray. And I want to build a home with you, wherever makes the most sense to be. Right now, that seems to be here, near Josh and Deena. My wolf likes being near enough to keep an eye on them. The maternal instinct doesn't go away just because your baby grows up."

"I'll have to work on my paternal instincts," Ray confided. "I never got to see Josh as a boy, so I'm starting fresh here with the young man he's become."

"I'm glad you got the chance," she told him, stroking his arm with gentle fingers. "And I'm glad you came back to me. I missed you." She couldn't say any more without sobbing, so she stopped there.

But Ray seemed to sense her mood, and he snuggled closer. His head bent down next to hers as he spoke near her ear. These words were just for the two of them.

"Each minute away from you was agony. I will never voluntarily leave your side again, my love. This is our time. For as long as we have together, I will cherish each moment, each breath, each sigh. You are my beloved and my one and only. Tonight, we start again. We've been wed in front of your people and mine. We have a new beginning."

Each of his words fell on her heart like a promise. The

strength of his arms around her gave her strength of will and clarity of vision. How she loved this man. This fey. This Knight.

Tears fell from her lashes, but they were tears of joy as she made a promise to him with her words. "You're right. We've been given a great gift—to start all over again. Let's make the most of it."

They kissed, and if magic swirled around them, it was easily contained by all the other mages present who had their backs. This moment was too significant to worry about anything other than the two of them. Together. Now...and forever.

EPILOGUE

"So, what about it?" Gabe sidled up to the pretty young werewolf woman, hoping she'd thawed a bit toward him. He couldn't help himself. Something about Margo spoke to him on a very basic level.

"What about what?" The look she gave him would have scorched ice.

So…she was going to make it difficult for him. Good. Gabe always liked a challenge.

"What about teaming up to find Bolivar?" he asked, reminding her about the conversation they'd had before the wedding where Ray had suggested they would make a good team.

"You think you can keep up with me?" Oh, yes. This little wolf woman was pressing all his buttons, probably hoping for a reaction.

She'd get one. Eventually. But it might not be the kind she expected. Gabe wondered what she'd think if he pulled her into his arms and kissed the challenging smile right off her face. The tantalizing idea almost made him try it, but he held back. He had to take things slow with this skittish creature.

Gabe allowed a tiny spark of his inner power to form a flame between his thumb and forefinger. Not enough magic use to draw unwanted attention from anyone who might be watching them a little too closely, but definitely enough of a showy display to make Margo's pretty brown eyes widen in surprise. Good. She looked intrigued.

"I can hold my own," he told her, casually snuffing out the magical flame in his hands. "And I like challenges."

He wondered if she realized he meant not only the challenge of tracking down a bad guy with unknown magical abilities, but also the challenge of getting into Margo's good graces—and her bed. Probably not. Not yet, anyway.

"All right." She faced him squarely. "Let's talk particulars tomorrow. I'm not saying I'll take you on just yet, but if I can get time off from my job, I'd like to do as Sir Rayburne suggested and go after Bolivar with just a small team."

"Two sounds like the perfect number to me," Gabe said, realizing he was pushing, but as with everything where this woman was concerned, he couldn't seem to help himself.

She eyed him through a skeptical squint. "We'll see about that."

# # #

ABOUT THE AUTHOR

Bianca D'Arc has run a laboratory, climbed the corporate ladder in the shark-infested streets of lower Manhattan, studied and taught martial arts, and earned the right to put a whole bunch of letters after her name, but she's always enjoyed writing more than any of her other pursuits. She grew up and still lives on Long Island, where she keeps busy with an extensive garden, several aquariums full of very demanding fish, and writing her favorite genres of paranormal, fantasy and sci-fi romance.

Bianca loves to hear from readers and can be reached through Twitter (@BiancaDArc), Facebook (BiancaDArcAuthor) or through the various links on her website.

WELCOME TO THE D'ARC SIDE...
WWW.BIANCADARC.COM

OTHER BOOKS BY BIANCA D'ARC

Brotherhood of Blood
One & Only
Rare Vintage
Phantom Desires
Sweeter Than Wine
Forever Valentine
Wolf Hills
Wolf Quest

Tales of the Were
Lords of the Were
Inferno

Tales of the Were ~
The Others
Rocky
Slade

Tales of the Were ~
String of Fate
Cat's Cradle
King's Throne
Jacob's Ladder
Her Warriors

Tales of the Were ~
Redstone Clan
The Purrfect Stranger
Grif
Red
Magnus
Bobcat
Matt

Tales of the Were ~
Grizzly Cove
All About the Bear
Mating Dance
Night Shift
Alpha Bear
Saving Grace
Bearliest Catch
The Bear's Healing Touch
The Luck of the Shifters
Badass Bear

Tales of the Were ~
Were-Fey Love Story
Lone Wolf
Snow Magic
Midnight Kiss

Tales of the Were ~
Jaguar Island (Howls)
The Jaguar Tycoon
The Jaguar Bodyguard

Gemini Project
Tag Team
Doubling Down

Resonance Mates
Hara's Legacy
Davin's Quest
Jaci's Experiment
Grady's Awakening
Harry's Sacrifice

The first three Grizzly Cove stories in one place!

Welcome to Grizzly Cove, where bear shifters can be who they are - if the creatures of the deep will just leave them be. Wild magic, unexpected allies, a conflagration of sorcery and shifter magic the likes of which has not been seen in centuries... That's what awaits the peaceful town of Grizzly Cove. That, and love. Lots and lots of love.

This anthology contains:

All About the Bear
Welcome to Grizzly Cove, where the sheriff has more than the peace to protect. The proprietor of the new bakery in town is clueless about the dual nature of her nearest neighbors, but not for long. It'll be up to Sheriff Brody to clue her in and convince her to stay calm—and in his bed—for the next fifty years or so.

Mating Dance
Tom, Grizzly Cove's only lawyer, is also a badass grizzly bear, but he's met his match in Ashley, the woman he just can't get out of his mind. She's got a dark secret, that only he knows. When ugliness from her past tracks her to her new home, can Tom protect the woman he is fast coming to believe is his mate?

Night Shift
Sheriff's Deputy Zak is one of the few black bear shifters in a colony of grizzlies. When his job takes him into closer proximity to the lovely Tina, though, he finds he can't resist her. Could it be he's finally found his mate? And when adversity strikes, will she turn to him, or run into the night? Zak will do all he can to make sure she chooses him.

Allie is about to discover a heritage of power…and blood…werecreatures, magic, and a misguided vampire who wants to kill two men who could be the loves of her life.

Allie was adopted. She had always known it, but when a mysterious older woman shows up and invites her to learn about her birth family, things take a turn for the odd.

Then Allie meets the Lords. Twin Alpha werewolves who rule over all North American were, Rafe and Tim may look exactly alike, but Allie can tell them apart from the moment they first meet. She's not sure what to think when they both want to claim her as their mate.

They are dominant, sexy, and all too ready to play games of the most delicious kind with her, but when a rogue vampire threatens her safety, they jump to her defense. It will take all of them working together, to stop the evil that has invaded their territory. Can they trust in each other and the power of their new love to prevail? Or will an ancient enemy win the day and usher evil incarnate back into the world?

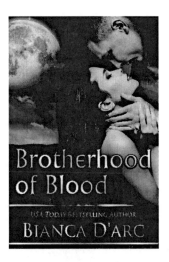

The first three novellas in the critically acclaimed vampire romance series, now in one place…

One & Only
Atticus is about to give up and greet the sun when he finds the love of his eternal life…by accident.

Rare Vintage
Marc, Master vampire of the Napa Valley, can't keep away from Kelly, no matter how many sparks fly between them. When an enemy challenges his authority, will she sacrifice her life for his?

Phantom Desires
Master Dmitri's lair is located under a farmhouse in rural Wyoming. Spying on the new owner while she sleeps could be more dangerous than even he suspects.

WWW.BIANCADARC.COM

CPSIA information can be obtained
at www.ICGtesting.com
Printed in the USA
LVOW10s1718101217
559295LV00009B/457/P